Changing Shape

Kathleen Wheeler

ACKNOWLEDGMENTS

This book wouldn't have come out nearly as well as it did without the help of some very special people. I'd like to take a moment here to thank them for all the inspiration, encouragement, support and friendship they've given me during this process.

Mom, thank you for your understanding and quiet encouragement; I hope I make you proud, even if it's not what I was supposed to have been doing.

Jillian Richardson, thank you for helping me get the nurses right, and for all your encouragement and positive energy.

Crystal Miller, thank you for your continued friendship and for being the perfect sounding board for my crazy ideas; this book definitely wouldn't have happened at all without you, even if it did change from that first concept.

Amy Craig- thank you for your years of friendship and for your encouragement with pretty much everything I do. Knowing you think I can helps me think I can and there's no way I can thank you for that; it would never be enough.

Carey S., Tara C., Amy M., and all the other beta readers out there that found the time to read even some of this and give me feedback- thank you.

Charryse, I don't know what to say. Thank you. You've given me so much for which I am grateful. I hope you are able to find your happy ending; I'm sorry it wasn't with me.

Lastly, I'd like to thank Elisa Gil-Pires, MD; who

out of all those mentioned here went well above and beyond what I could ever have hoped for. Elisa, even with everything going on in your life you were somehow able to find the time to answer my thousand and one medical questions, read the rough draft, provide notes, pointers, explanations and encouragement…I can't even begin to thank you for what you've given to me just by being you.

Thank you to all of you, I cherish our friendships and look forward to many more years of laughter and tears with you.

Changing Shape

DEDICATION

For Marion.

And for Katie.

And for John, Kristen and Karyn.

I know this doesn't touch it, but I hope it does an honor.

Chapter 1

There's no such thing as silence in the city; what a comforting thought. No matter what the hour there is always someone coming home or heading out or dogs barking or trashcans being overturned or car alarms or the gentle whir that buildings make or the swoosh of air from the trains beneath the streets, or the city crews taking advantage of the near emptiness to keep up the façade of order, perhaps it's the cooing of pigeons or the squealing of rats or the distant roar of an airplane overhead or just the rustling of the breeze blowing trash around. Even in a clean city somehow there's always trash for the wind to kick up. And I love it here, despite the noise and because of it; it's alive, with a pulse of its own. Here I can be somebody and nobody at the same time; where the biggest of my foibles is mundane, and even all by myself I'm never completely alone.

It didn't take Elizabeth Thornton long to get used to the noise of Boston, having moved straight from the student apartments at UNC Chapel Hill where she accomplished her MBA at the Kenan-Flagler Business School. But the quiet has always been something that she cherished even if it's not the kind of quiet she grew up with. These days, the closest thing to silence she could find was on her daily run. Five miles rain or shine, when the only thing she had to focus on was the intake and expiration of air into her lungs, the sound and feel of her feet pounding out a rhythm against the road or the treadmill, when the loudest thought she had was the blood screaming through her veins and her own heart beat competing with the music faithfully strapped to her arm.

It was in this hour and a half routine every day that she could relax and forget all the pressures of being the youngest and only female Senior VP at the prestigious Boston advertising firm Gordon Phillips; with its 12 to 14 hour days and near continuously revolving door of trouble-shooting and deadlines and headaches. Forget about not having had a real date in over a year because she hadn't had the time or energy. Forget about growing up an awkward only child to a single mother in a small town, feeling like an outcast. Forget that she'd never really been in love. It was only the steady rhythm of her feet and her heart and her breathing and the sensations of activity to carry her from one moment to the next; that's all that mattered out here on the road.

The sky had been steadily brightening, the soft twilight glow of pre-dawn becoming more harsh and alive as the first edge of the sun peeked up over the horizon and night officially became day. Elizabeth slowed her pace to a walk, checked her heart rate monitor and the hammering pulse in her neck and began the arm stretches that marked the beginning of her cool down. Breathing heavily but controlled, she inhaled the salty sea air mixed with the smell of cars and concrete, the trace of dirt and the new plants of spring faint but present in the air. *Man, it's good to be alive!* It was early-April and the snow had finally melted, but it was still cold enough that her breath came out in thick puffs of steam. There was a blanket of fog dancing atop the Charles River and the early morning crew teams were stealthy silhouettes of grace and speed skimming across the glassy surface of the water.

She had always envied those who did team sports; herself always having been too shy and awkward to participate in much, but always wanting to be a part of something, to be popular. All through school, when she wasn't at the bakery helping her mother, she could usually be found in the library with her nose in a book. And not always because there was reading assigned, but because she was genuinely interested in whatever she was reading. Over time this gave her a reputation for being aloof, and in fact she was, often relating better to books than to her peers for several reasons.

Throughout her time in the Carbondale Community School System, she was made fun of. Not only for her bookish ways but also because of her second hand wardrobe and her lack of a father. Some days, it was because she was the tallest girl in her grade, despite also being the youngest having skipped two for being so smart which probably did the most to alienate her since she fit in neither with her academic peers nor within her own age group. This was most pronounced in middle and high school, when all the other kids were hitting puberty and began dating; in this, she was always painfully behind.

On the social scale, she was only slightly ahead of Theresa Fitzgerald who peed in her seat in the second grade or poor Stanley Wright who had had lice in the fourth and gave it to half the class. Despite this, she was always one of the very last to be picked for anything sports related. This had everything to do with the fact that she was the least coordinated kid on the playground having had several growth spurts that finally landed her at 6'1" by the time she was a senior. She was always trying to get a handle on her limbs, never quite getting caught up to them, and by the time she stopped growing, it was too late. Stanley and Theresa at least didn't trip over their own feet and knew where their hands were to catch with.

It didn't matter that her mother seemed to be

well liked and a successful community business owner or that they didn't need for any of the important stuff. Maybe the other kids had it hard at home and needed a way to feel better about their own lives. Maybe they just wanted to slide by unnoticed and either remained silent or joined in so that they didn't get the brunt of it themselves. Kids rarely bother to look beneath the surface where usually the most beautiful things are found. None of it makes it alright, but it at least makes it a little more understandable. It doesn't serve you well to stand out; even the prettiest girl in the room is hated by those in her shadow.

She never did know which came first between retreating into books or getting teased; she figured it was probably a bit of both and didn't give it too much thought anymore; things simply were they way they were. She always had her mother's love and that was all that mattered in the grand scheme of things.

It wasn't until junior year in college that she really began to hit her stride, when her age caught up with her place. A couple successful years with good grades and a growing circle of friends had boosted her self confidence. Add to that a few flings and experiments that were progressively less and less awkward and Elizabeth Thornton was finally out of her shell, her insecurities shoved tightly into the vault of things that made up her old self as she found a way to reinvent who she was.

She ended the walking portion of her trek back at the entryway to her building and gathered up the newspapers waiting for her there. She punched in her security code and took the stairs up to her fifth floor apartment by twos, still riding the endorphins coursing through her blood stream. Once inside, she pulled her iPhone from its armband, placed it in the recharging dock and put the newspapers on the table nearby. No sooner was she in her apartment then did her mind begin to race through her multitude of to-do lists. While her mind was thinking ahead to what she'd wear and deciding what to buy Jennifer for Administrative Professional day, she opened her entryway closet and removed her heart rate monitor, chest strap, running shoes, and armband placing it all just inside the door on the floor and shelf designated for these items, the actions rendered rote by repetition.

She then moved through the apartment to the kitchen and removed the hip pack that carried her water and snacks placing it on the counter and rinsing out the water bottle leaving it in the dish rack to dry. As she toweled off her hands, she contemplated breakfast and decided on a toasted English muffin with a mashed banana as spread. She went to the fridge to pour herself a glass of orange juice and she took it all with her into the master bathroom where she turned on some music and proceeded make a quick loop around the master suite to ensure that all the laundry from the previous evening and morning was arranged in their correct bins.

She opened the glass door to her shower and turned the water on. While she was waiting for the steam to pour out of the enclosure telling her it was warm, she stripped off her clothes and put them in the hamper. On her way back to the shower, she caught a glimpse of herself in the full length mirror and stopped to examine the reflection; this was something that she didn't usually do. Not that she was uncomfortable with herself or with her own nudity – she just didn't think about it that often. She examined her long trim frame, her medium build with stretched out limbs and a torso proportionate to the rest. She turned to the side and looked appraisingly at the flatness of her stomach, the pert roundness of her full breasts, the gentle rise and slope of her ass and the slight curve of her hip. She noticed the lean muscles in her arms and legs, alternately flexing each to see better the lines of definition.

Her skin was milky and smooth, dappled sparingly by a smattering of freckles that almost perfectly matched her strawberry blond curls. *You're looking pretty hot there, Elle- We gotta get you laid.* At this thought she crinkled her nose, stuck her tongue out at herself and ran to the now steaming shower not wanting to think about how utterly lacking that part of her life had been since she broke it off with Colin, regardless the few one-nighters she'd managed to pick up since.

Colin was a great guy and all, good looking, successful and fit; there just wasn't that spark she was looking for, which seemed to be missing from all of her relationships lately. Life in college and grad school was so much simpler and love was easier to find, even if it wasn't the forever kind.

Sex with Colin was just okay, and she often had to either fake it or help herself to climax either during or after the fact. But, it was easier with him than it was to find a willing no-strings tryst that was outside her social or professional circles, one that for a few hours at least might actually fulfill what her body needed. Not really a reason to carry on a basically unfulfilling relationship, but it's during these dry spells that she began to wonder what must be the matter with her that she hasn't been able to find 'the one' yet. And did she even really want to?

Chapter 2

"Are you sure you need me to do this? This is part of why I made you CEO, Manning- so I wouldn't have to deal with all this publicity shit," Hailey Jensen said with unveiled exasperation and defeat. She was sitting on her couch with her head resting on the back, looking at the ceiling wishing it would open up a black hole to suck her up into oblivion. Throughout her childhood and into her late twenties Hailey had essentially lived her life according to Phillip Jensen's plans for his daughter. She attended the best private schools, went to the best colleges, travelled in the best circles and dated the right boys; all things designed by her father to groom her for the life generations of Jensens had worked hard at one thing or another to get and maintain. All the same things that he'd had to do in his turn and his parents before him and so on. That was how it was with long rich families; it's just as much about the image of power as it is actual net worth. But for all the pomp and circumstance involved in being a Jensen, there was real love and real warmth between her father and herself. She wanted to please him, even at the expense of herself, and he was never more proud than day she came to work with him at Jensen Industries Incorporated.

When her mother suddenly up and left them for her personal trainer without a backward glance Hailey was 9 and it had shocked and devastated both her father and herself. It hadn't been long on the heels of the accident that left her older brother Fitch brain damaged and in a wheelchair, destined to live out his days at a care facility unable to understand beyond the level of a

4 year old. He was 17 when it happened. 6 years later he died from a clot leaving her as the only heir.

Hailey understood now that her mother had probably shattered that day making everything that remained into a reminder of what had been lost and the guilt of having been the one behind the wheel, but it still didn't excuse the fact that she abandoned her daughter and husband. In the long run, Hailey and her father had been made closer by those dark times, each needing the other even more. Phillip showed his strength and love by making himself more available for his daughter rather than hiding from his pain by burying himself in his work as so many in similar situations often do. Even so, Hailey had often wished to have her mother; in those moments when talking to her father was awkward or she just needed a mother's love. She had cried until she had no more tears to spare for Whitney Hobarthe-Jensen.

On the surface, Hailey did everything that was expected of a privileged young lady of her station, but inside she was dying to break free. She had fought hard to get her father to allow her to attend art school and he only did so with the concession that she simultaneously obtained a business degree. When she discovered that she preferred the company of women to the boys and young men that her father was setting her up with, she kept it to herself not wanting to disappoint his ideas of future generations. He may have suspected something when she summarily dismissed every single one of these potential boyfriends before things got far along, but he continued to try.

She hated the fakery and pretension that made up the social circles she was forced to participate in and she hated herself for playing along with it. She loved her father, and believed that he loved her as well. But there was always a small part of her that was afraid she'd somehow lose him too so she continued the charade for him, while living as herself on the side in secret. When he died it just confirmed her suspicion, even though in her head she knew that it wasn't the same- he didn't leave her on purpose the way her mother had.

Through his death, Hailey inherited JII and all its subsidiaries, a vast fortune, quite a few pieces of prime real estate including the estate in Atherton and several modes of transportation. Hailey would have given it all away to have her family back.

"Look Hails," His voice softened. Peter Manning had been Hailey's best friend since her father first hired his parents to manage his household after her mother left. "I know you never enjoyed doing these events, and I understand how much harder they are now that your dad's gone; hell I miss him too- he was like an uncle to me. But this isn't one you can just skip, and you know it. You're donating a park to the city in his name and you have to be there at the presentation and the ground breaking and you have to make an appearance at the cocktail social after. You don't have to stay for that, but you have to at least show up. You can be my date."

She could imagine him wiggling his eyebrows in mock salaciousness and she let out a guffaw. It had been a long running joke between them for years, made funnier by the fact that Peter was also gay. If it hadn't been for the fact that they were raised together practically as siblings in the same household they might have made the perfect beards for each other, a trick that had only worked for a short time in school. Despite hard times in high school with one particular bully that couldn't accept the lust Peter inspired in him, he didn't really need a cover story since his station in life afforded him so much more freedom. A fact that Hailey often thought for many reasons was unfair- not that he had more freedom, but the entire idea of class; the stupid idea that someone's lineage or financial status has any bearing on their general worth as a human being rankled her deeply. Although many in her circles saw Peter as nothing more than the progeny of 'the help,' the Jensens came to see the Mannings as part of their family and Peter became a sort of surrogate son for Phillip and his mother provided the female wisdom that she craved and at times required. Peter's father Paul grew to be an uncle figure for Hailey and when her father died a few years ago, this relationship became even more important.

"What would Michael say?" She laughed.

"It's good to hear you laugh." She could hear the smile in his voice. "You know Michael knows the deal. It's you and me 'til the bitter end, Baby. Thick and thin, just like always."

She suddenly turned serious. "I love you, Peta. You're my best friend and I don't know what I'd have done without you. You know that right?" She fought to keep her voice steady as tears threatened.

"I know. I am pretty fabulous." She laughed. "I love you too, you know. I'll see you Thursday. Do you want me to send a car or pick you up myself?"

"Can you get away?"

"Anything for you, Hails…You know she'll probably be there, right?"

"I thought you were trying to convince me to go, not run me off."

"I'm just giving you fair warning, Honey. She is a climbing asshat and she was a shit to you. She never deserved your love in the first place and she definitely doesn't deserve even a thought from you now." His tone was almost angry he was so serious and this warmed her.

"I know. She doesn't even deserve the energy it's taking to talk about her right now, you're right. But you know how hard it was for me, to lose her so soon after dad died. Besides why she left me- and how I found out- the timing couldn't possibly have been worse and that's the part that hurt the most. I just hate her and everyone like her, which unfortunately is most of the people that are going to be at this thing."

"Hey – I'll be there. And Michael will be there. Besides, you can always bring Zoë."

"She's just a friend and you know that."

"She's one of the sexiest women I've ever met, Hailey and she's crazy about you, in case you haven't noticed. I've known this since you first started hanging out with her back in Rhode Island. I don't know why you can't take it to the next level with her – the sex is good, right?"

Purposely ignoring his question, "You know why, Peta. I'm not having this conversation right now, and I don't want to lead Zoë on by flying her out to California like that. She's my friend and that's all I need or want right now."

"You can't let that cunt Genevieve ruin your chance to find real love. If it's not Zoë, I hope at least you'll keep an open mind when you do meet the one?" He sounded hopeful, but he knew from having this same conversation so many times before that it was always a long shot.

"Jesus, Peter! Tell me how you really feel!" She laughed then sobered. "When I'm ready, I'll try to keep an open mind, I promise. But really, what's the point in loving anyone when all they do is leave?"

Chapter 3

At 7:30am Elizabeth stepped off the elevator and entered the offices of Gordon Phillips, two steaming venti mocha lattes and her red Jack Georges briefcase in hand. She was wearing a charcoal grey tailored skirt suit with a pond-moss green silk shell beneath a belted Burberry trench coat. Her shoulder length strawberry blonde curls were left loose this day and her minimalist approach to makeup left her face looking fresh and clean with just a hint of wine tinted lip balm staining her lips and a touch of shadow on her eyelids to accentuate the almond shape and emerald irises. Just enough femininity to downplay her intimidating size, made all the more so by the heels of her Jimmy Choo shoes clicking smartly on the granite floor.

In exchange for a pile of mail and messages, she handed one of the coffees to her executive assistant, Jennifer. "Good morning Jennifer- I hope you like chocolate in your coffee."

"Oh you know I do and good morning to you, Elizabeth. Happy Tuesday." Jennifer happily accepted the drink with a wide smile that showed off her perfectly straight white teeth and a nod of thanks, her simple pony tail bobbing up and down. Jennifer was in her middle twenties, a recent graduate of Boston College with a BS in Management and Leadership. This was her first official job outside of internships, but she came with several notable letters of recommendation, so when Elizabeth's previous EA left the position because her husband got transferred to Japan, Elizabeth took a shot and has been thanking her luck ever since.

Jennifer had been a valuable asset to her team both as a worker and as a person, catching on quickly and taking on more and more responsibility. She was someone Elizabeth trusted, and Elizabeth knew that someday she would have to promote her to a role that really exploited all of the young woman's talents. *That will be a bittersweet day- losing the best assistant I could ask for to create the position of Strategic Account Manager. Hmmm…that's not a bad idea, actually. Change Jennifer's title and pay grade and give the two of us someone to keep the gate and run reports. If Alethea goes through this morning, Harry will be in a good enough headspace to approve this and I can make the announcement at the employee appreciation event in a couple weeks…*

Jennifer handed her a quite hefty stack of files, papers and envelopes effectively breaking Elizabeth out of her thoughts. "Here is your mail, Elizabeth."

"What's on the agenda for today? Is there anything pressing that I should know about?" Coffee and notebook in hand, Jennifer followed Elizabeth into her office.

Reading from one of the legal pads where she wrote down everything most urgent, "Mr. Gordon is expecting you to present the latest Alethea campaign changes- that's going to be in conference room C at 10:00."

At this, Elizabeth rolled her eyes and flashed a quick retching expression, which made Jennifer giggle. They both had spent several late nights together in the last couple weeks scrambling to arrange significant changes to a couple Alethea projects that were already well under way. Luckily, or unluckily depending on how one looked at it, Alethea was a multi product, multi channel, multi million dollar account so it didn't matter that their Chief Marketing Officer was a prick blowhard who wouldn't even try to understand the first thing about effective advertising in the modern age. *At least their marketing team is young and open to fresh ideas, maybe he's up for retirement soon…*

"Did we get the final proofs back from the printer?"

"Yes, they're right here," She indicated a large black folio leaning against the desk end opposite where Elizabeth was standing, "waiting for the final once over from you to make sure they're in the correct order. Then I can take them to the conference room for you and set them up."

Elizabeth raised an eyebrow in acknowledgement while scanning through the documents in her hand, sorting them into piles on her desk. "That's great, Jennifer. Thanks. What else?"

Noting the approval in her boss's expression Jennifer returned her attention to her notebook. "Yes. You have a luncheon scheduled with Barbara Mullins from MassPower to go over the preliminaries of their rebranding initiative; you're meeting her at 12:30 at Lou's. Did you want me to schedule a car?"

"Yes, Please. That would be great."

"Also, you wanted me to remind you to hand the Peter Jacobs account over to John Schultz. He's scheduled to swing by your office around 3 for that. I've already started printing the related emails and pulling all the documentation for it and should have that ready for you before lunch." Jennifer relayed a few more things and finally put the end of her pencil near the corner of her mouth and scanned the page again to make sure she hadn't left anything out.

"Ok, that sounds great Jennifer, thank you. Can you book a small venue for a team appreciation luncheon at the end of the month and get it organized? Noon to 3 should be good; any of the regular places will be fine. I'd also like to have some bubbly if this deal goes through. That will certainly be cause to celebrate."

~~~

"We all know that consumers formulate their brand awareness and determine intent to purchase through multiple channels including major media- that's nothing new. However, just because major media is 'old news,'" she scrunched her fingers in the universal sign for air quotes, "television and print is still the best way to reach the majority of the American audience, especially customers in the flyover states and those in the older age groups. Television and magazines specifically are a must for us to market your products effectively – especially in the short term." Elizabeth addressed the conference room, an hour into the presentation, talking with her hands to push her point across. Her confidence is charisma and there was just enough flirtation to keep the clients at ease. So far the ideas presented had been well received and Elizabeth had been able to answer all the questions with grace and ease. This was her element- her wheelhouse, as it were. As with most potential clients, it took weeks of back and forth, market analysis and strategizing for the most effective variegated program with a multiphase rollout to ensure long term success for the client. Late nights spent with take-out dinners, both alone and with the team, pouring over demographics and sales numbers and similar product case studies to determine what had worked in the past, complete with reasonable projections and troubleshooting solutions options.

Her confidence high, she was utterly convinced that she had relayed the best possible solution and it showed in the ease with which she discussed it. She'd done her homework and even if the client either didn't like every idea or had ideas of their own, she had the tools in place to make it work for them.

"We at Gordon Phillips will reinforce the traditional methodologies by incorporating alternative communication channels including social media and web promotions as vehicles for engaging your tech savvy audience- your coastal and millennial customers- in an interactive and trackable manner. This interaction will provide a platform that will enable direct communication to your consumer, a better understanding of who that consumer is and what products are creating the "raving fan" versus the passive purchaser. The highlight here is this side of the launch will provide extensive trackable raw data streams. We will run these data streams through our nationally recognized data team here at Gordon Phillips to find and maximize the niche markets that are flying under the radar."

After taking a sip of water she continued, "Once these solutions are in place, new product rollout and promotion will be a snap. When new products launch, under the Gordon Phillips solution there will be a sense of brand cohesion between new and old. Which, and correct me if I'm wrong here, but having a new product launch that is immediately recognizable as Alethea and leveraging that household name would be paramount to success. At Gordon Phillips we accomplish that every day for our clients."

Making strong eye contact with each of Alethea's team she drove it home. "We want to be Alethea's partner in this. At Gordon Phillips we do not create singular ad campaigns to get some toasters and screwdrivers out to market for a quick cash fix. We create strategies to increase unaided brand awareness. We partner because when you become a Gordon Phillips client you become part of our brand family. This sense of community and pride we have for our current clients will be immediately leveraged for the Koken and Cardinal Tools brands. This is not what you will get with some of the larger firms. Our buying power and connections lends us the same muscle that they have, but our smaller size and core values allows us to be more flexible and sensitive to your needs. Gordon Phillips is the partner you need to move Alethea's business forward."

With this she closed her presentation packet and determined that there weren't any further questions. She glanced at Harry Gordon who had a slight grin on his face, his eyes sparkling with approval.

David Cabot, Alethea CMO and general all around douche-bag, surprised both Elizabeth and Harry by saying, "It sounds like a good plan, and your numbers appear solid- actually more realistic than some of the other ad agencies we've been talking to. I like your ideas and I think I can confidently tell you now that we want to work with Gordon Phillips on this."

It was not without some difficulty, but both Harry and Elizabeth managed not to stare with their mouths open for more than a second or two before smiling.

Harry took David's outstretched hand and shook

it firmly, "That's wonderful news, David. We look forward to getting this campaign launched. I'll have the contracts over to you by the end of this week." Hand shakes all around and Elizabeth was already starting to rise high on the rush of another big win.

This is what it was all about. The culmination of all those long hours of hard work, the late nights, the strategy meetings and back and forth to hone the perfect deal came down to this one moment, the climax akin to a cocaine high without the crash, or sex or surviving an insane rollercoaster. The increased pulse rate, the adrenaline and dopamine coursing, the flush of heat on the skin and the feeling of invincibility; no wonder they say winning is addictive.

Schooling her features to something hopefully resembling neutrally pleased, she left the group and headed back to her office to check in before her lunch meeting. As she approached Jennifer's cubicle, Jennifer looked up and asked, "So how did it go?"

Nearly giddy from excitement, Elizabeth beckoned her into her office and told her, "We got it!" and they shared a moment of practically jumping up and down for joy.

Chapter 4

"Hey Patty – Here let me help you with that." Hailey rushed over to the middle aged woman who was struggling with an armload of boxes while trying to open a door and relieved her of some of her burden, tucking it under an arm and reaching for the door.

"Oh hey yourself Hailey- thanks." She let out a puff of air, "I'm glad you came along when you did." Patty led Hailey in through the bakery's back door and into the offices where she deposited her boxes onto the desk and indicated for Hailey to do the same. She pushed a lock of her red curls off her face and asked with a smile, "What brings you into town?"

"Well, I wanted to see my good friend before heading out on a business trip for a few days, see if maybe she needed any help with anything before I go. Looks like I showed up just in the nick of time." She pointed to the boxes and smiled warmly at Patty who returned the affectionate expression with ease.

"That you did, my friend." She opened one of the boxes and pulled out a blue ball cap with the River Rock Bakery logo emblazoned on the front and tossed it to Hailey. "If that's not a good color for you there's green, red and white too – but I think that blue goes with your eyes."

"Oh Patty – this is so cool! Are you going to sell these out in the shop?"

"Yep. They're getting added to the uniform for the employees and then we'll put some out to sell along with the reusable grocery sacks that are in that box there," she indicated the other box for Hailey to open.

"Take one of those too if you want – I can always use the free advertising." She laughed.

"I can't take all your merchandise, Patty – I will keep the hat though." She smiled and put it on her head and adjusted the fit.

"So you're headed out on a business trip, huh? Want me to check on your house while you're gone?"

"If you don't mind just swinging by and making sure no one's out there messing around I'd appreciate it. I'll leave the alarms on, though so if we get another freeze before spring sets in for good you'll have to deactivate them to get inside if you need to. I don't expect any trouble and I'll only be gone 'til Sunday, so it should be OK left alone, but you never know."

"Alrighty, then- it's not a problem for me at all. You know Riley and I walk out that way most evenings anyway, so it's not a big deal for us."

She nodded her understanding and smiled in appreciation. "Well, I've gotta go run a few errands before I head out tomorrow- are we still on for dinner tonight?"

"It's Wednesday, isn't it?" She chuckled. "You know I look forward all week to our Wednesdays, right?"

"Yea, me too." She flashed a brilliant smile. "Ok then – you want me to pick up anything special while I'm out?"

"Nope- it's my turn to cook and I've got some meat marinating in the fridge as we speak."

"Ok then, sounds good. I'll see you around six." She got up to leave and Patty rose as well, and walked her through the kitchen and to the front of the store.

She grabbed one of her employees on the way.

"Hey Tami – can you please help out Hailey here – just write it down on the dropped sheet." She raised a hand to stop Hailey's protest, "I insist. I happen to know the owner of this fine establishment and she owes me a favor or two." She winked at them and turned back toward her office.

"There's just no arguing with her, is there?" Hailey muttered amusedly.

"No ma'am. She's one tough cookie." Tami stated with equal amusement. "Your usual?"

"Yea, that's fine, but you're letting me pay."

Chapter 5

"Jennifer, can you come in here please?" Elizabeth was sitting at her desk looking at her monitor and as Jennifer entered the room she clicked a few windows shut and stood. Gesturing with her hand, she indicated the sofa and wingback chairs that comprised a warm seating area in a corner of her large office. "Let's sit over here. Can you close the door please?"

Closing the door behind her Jennifer turned a quizzical eye to her boss and asked, "What's up?"

"I just wanted to have a chat with you, I feel like we've been so busy that we haven't had much of a chance to catch up and there are a couple things I wanted to run by you."

They sat on opposite ends of the couch, their bodies turned to face each other as they spoke. After some preliminary small talk to ease into the conversation Elizabeth said, "So, Jennifer. You've been with us here at Gordon Phillips for what? Nearly 2 years?"

"Yes, that's right. I've been here for 1 year and 8 months on the eighteenth." She shifted her body slightly on the couch, curious as to where this conversation was going and unsure she wanted to know.

"Do you feel as though being my Assistant is challenging all of your faculties?" Elizabeth was watching Jennifer's body language and subtle changes in expression, enjoying the internal squirming that the younger woman was trying to hide. This was another part of her job that Elizabeth enjoyed. Knowing that she held the power to change the lives of her employees and using that power for good felt good. *Let's make her work for it, though...there's not much fun in just handing something over.*

"It certainly has its moments that's for sure." At this she chuckled lightly. "I enjoy being part of a team. I like having an important role and I enjoy being in a position where I'm relied upon by not only you but also the rest of the team to some extent. It makes me feel connected to the projects and a vital part of what's going on here. It doesn't hurt that I have a great boss who helps to make me feel valuable by asking my opinion and taking me seriously. That's worth a lot." With this, she placed her hands back onto her lap and slightly shifted her position on the couch again.

Elizabeth turned the corner of her mouth up slightly and cocked her head a bit and asked, "Where do you see yourself going from here?" Once the question was past her lips she kicked one of her shoes off and brought that leg up to tuck it more underneath her, glad that she wore pants this day.

Jennifer's eyes widened slightly at this question, and she had to work to keep the apprehension from settling onto her brow. "What do you mean?"

To ease some of the tension she could see on Jennifer's face, she raised her hands slightly and gestured palms out in a placating manner. "I just mean that you graduated with high marks from a good school with a degree in management; it seems when you chose that as a major you didn't really see yourself as someone's assistant. I'm curious to know what your plans for yourself are, that's all."

Relaxing somewhat, Jennifer replied, "Well, as

someone fairly fresh out of school I understand that you can't get there in one step, but I certainly see myself ending up in more of a leadership role, with my own staff, running a department or company…more like what you do. Right now, I look at what I'm doing as a learning experience and I'm having a great time doing it."

"I'm really glad to hear that Jennifer and I certainly appreciate all your hard work." She looked Jennifer directly in the eye, her expression warm. "In fact, I've created the position of Strategic Accounts Manager specifically for you, if you're interested. Of course, this means more responsibility, higher pay and we'll have to find another Admin, but if you're game, I'm very pleased to offer it to you."

"Are you serious?" Jennifer's exuberance nearly propelled her off the couch. Her eyes widened considerably and she was smiling almost goofily and nodding her head.

Nodding and smiling in return Elizabeth told her, "The details of the position still need to be hammered out, but we should have that all pinned down by the time we hire your replacement. Essentially I see you in a similar role as the one you have now, working directly with me to make sure projects go smoothly, to ensure that the needs of the team are addressed and to coordinate with the different team leads and departments so that the deadlines are met and so forth. Someone else can do the more administrative secretarial type stuff."

Jennifer was listening raptly, her eyes sparkling. "As the SAM, you will require a strong understanding of what the client expectations are, which means you will be dealing with them in a more direct capacity, which will give you an opportunity to see some of the sales side as we set these projects up as well as when their needs change or as the relationship grows.

"I see a lot of potential in you, Jennifer and I believe this new position will better leverage your talents and get you in a better place for advancement for the future."

"This is amazing news Elizabeth. I can't begin to thank you enough for this opportunity." Her ponytail bobbed back and forth as Jennifer shook her head in near disbelief. "I won't let you down."

Elizabeth moved to stand up and Jennifer mimicked the movement. They hugged and as Jennifer headed toward the door Elizabeth let her know, "We'll make the announcement at the team lunch later today. HR has all the details and they should be in touch with you within the next few days to go over it all and get your signature on a few things. In the meantime, we'll need to post the Admin opening so we can get you replaced ASAP. Since we'll be sharing the new assistant somewhat, I'd like you to do the resume culling and prescreening interviews and set me up with your top 3 or 4 picks. You can get that process started in the morning."

Elizabeth waved her on and turned back to her desk to get a few things done before the team lunch. Jennifer exited the office with an extra spring in her step, smiling to herself and feeling on top of the world.

Chapter 6

"Hailey! Over here." Peter Manning stood a lanky six-foot-two waving his hand in the air trying to get Hailey's attention. He was wearing a pair of khaki cargo shorts and a baby blue polo shirt. His Ray-Bans were looped into the v at his neck and he looked like a fashion plate with his mouse brown hair swept around his head in an attempt to look nonchalant; this was enhanced by his two days worth of scruff and flip-flopped feet. He looked even more tanned than he did last time Hailey saw him and for a second she was a bit jealous, never having been able to reach that level of bronzed herself for her fair skin.

"Hey Peta-bo-beeta!" She dropped her bags when she reached him and jumped into his waiting arms giving him a big hug which was returned with equal verve.

"Hey Hailsy-bells," He held her at arms length and inspected her. "Lookin' good, hot stuff- what say we blow this popsicle stand?"

"Lead the way, oh brother from a better mother."

He picked up her luggage and together they walked out of the airport and into the short term parking area where they retrieved Peter's Silver Range Rover Evoque.

Hailey raised an eyebrow at him. "Oh don't you start on me too. I get enough flack for this car from Mom and Dad I don't need it from you too." His tone was light and filled with humor, belying the harshness of his words. Then he leaned in conspiratorially, "It is a little ostentatious, though isn't it?"

Hailey just laughed. "I didn't say a thing."

"Well you know, my favorite car is still that little Chevy your dad gave me in college, but it's not really appropriate for the CEO of a multibillion dollar global company to tool around in a beater, now is it?" He looked sidelong at her for a few seconds and then added, "It's good to see you Hails. I've missed you."

She reached over and patted him on the shoulder, "I've missed you too, Peta."

"Mom's expecting us for dinner tonight. Did you want to drop this stuff at the house now and get settled in or did you want to head straight over?"

"You can just take me to the main house, Peta. I'll take a shower and change and then I'll just head over."

"You know, you can stay with Michael and me if you want…you don't have to stay in that big old empty house all by yourself."

"I know, and I appreciate that Pete I really do. This is my home; it's where I grew up. I can't just avoid it forever." She sat quietly looking out the window as the traffic began to shift and thicken again. Even though it wasn't really home anymore, it was still her house and she'd be damned if a few memories would keep her from enjoying it for the few days she would be there.

"Well, let me know if you change your mind." He maneuvered the SUV onto the exit ramp and navigated the surface roads from the freeway to the sprawling Jensen estate, where they stopped to enter the gate code and drove the circular drive to the house.

Peter parked the car and was pulling Hailey's bags out from the trunk area when the large front door of the house opened and the elder Mannings rushed out to greet them.

"Hailey! Oh it's so good to see you!" Evelyn Manning had been the closest thing to a mother Hailey had since her own left her so long ago and it always warmed Hailey's heart to see her. She wrapped Hailey in a big hug and gave her a hearty squeeze, "It's been too long, you know." She chided in a loving tone into Hailey's hair.

"I know Ama, I've missed you too."

Paul Manning gave Hailey a warm hug, welcomed her home and held her at arms length. "Still as beautiful as ever- I guess all that mountain air must be good for something. It's been too quiet without you, you know." He sniffed and looked away, not wanting to let his emotions show too openly. Paul Manning was a proud man and his British roots and years of butler training dictated a certain air of decorum, but Hailey recognized the love she felt from this man. He was one of the few people she could truly count on and she adored him for it.

"It's nice to see you too, Paul." She squeezed his shoulder.

"Right. Well come on Peter, let's get the bags into the house. The day's not getting any brighter and nothing's getting done with us standing here." He grabbed the biggest bag and wheeled it into the house.

That evening the Manning's small home was filled with love and the camaraderie that exists within family; it warmed Hailey's heart and for the first time since her father died she was comfortable being home.

Instead of feeling guilty for enjoying the love of these wonderful people who had adopted her into their hearts as one of their own when her own blood was so far away, she allowed herself to feel soothed by it again. It was around ten in the evening when Paul and Evelyn both started to fade and retired for the night. Peter and Hailey took this as their cue and went to their respective homes.

On the short walk between the Manning's home and her own house Hailey once more reflected on the events of the last several months and felt the heaviness in her chest finally beginning to ease; rather than the acute oppression and the crushing weight caused by yet another deep loss in her life she instead felt an ache that was beginning to dull and allow some perspective in. When she realized this, it was hard not to allow the guilt wash over her at the relief the revelation had caused.

When she arrived at her back yard, she noted that the cover was off the pool and decided a few laps would be just the remedy for any lingering feelings of sadness threatening to curl their dark fingers around her heart and squeeze. She stripped down to her skin and swam until her limbs could no longer propel her forward and then continued to float for a while before dragging herself in to bed.

Chapter 7

Saturday started the same as most of her Saturdays began. Elizabeth awoke alone in her bed, her eyes blinking open slowly as the early morning sunlight poked through the cracks of space around the heavy curtains hanging in her picture window. She rolled over onto her side and reached to face the clock toward her and see what time it was: 8:13, time to get up.

As she headed into the bathroom for her morning routine, she was thinking about all the things she'd like to get done before she met some friends in Cambridge for a night on the town. Already she was making a list.

After she pat her face dry, she walked into her large closet and chose the running clothes she'd don that morning starting the process of getting dressed. As always, she made sure that her night clothes made it into the laundry bin; secretly feeling guilty that she required people to do her house work for her when she's a fully functioning adult, not wanting to make them to have to work too hard despite the tidy sum she paid.

After her run, she returned home, showered and dressed for the day. It was unseasonably warm out and she decided to wear a few lighter layers rather than one heavy one. She picked out a pair of not too obscenely low-rise skinny jeans that hugged her hips like the gentle caress of a lover and made her legs look even longer than they already were, a body hugging white v-neck tank beneath a rose colored henley and topped it off with a black zip-up hoodie. She added her favorite pair of PF Flyers high-tops to complete the ensemble.

In the main living area, she wrote a quick note to Claudia, her cleaning lady, giving her instructions for the day. She then jotted down a quick grocery list placing it next to her keys and phone and she moved to take the wallet insert out that contained her ID and debit card, placing it in her pocket and her bag into the closet which she proceeded to lock. Claudia hasn't given her any reason for distrust but Elizabeth had always been cautious in this way. *You can't get burned if you don't tempt the flames.*

On her way to the grocery store she called her friend Jane. Jane and her partner Robert had standing plans with Elizabeth and several other friends every Saturday to go to the cooking school where they met once a week to prepare and exchange a week's worth of meals together. On the rare occasion that Elizabeth couldn't make it because she'd had to travel for work Jane and Robert compensated and delivered.

This was one of the few things that Elizabeth looked forward to all week long, and she felt blessed to have such great friends to share this with. During the week she worked very hard, often long hours and didn't have much time for every day living type things which is why she had a house keeper and a laundry service. And she loved to cook; ever since she was a young girl when her mother was testing recipes for the bakery Elizabeth relished in helping out. When she told her mother that she wanted to cook dinners for her a couple nights a week to help lighten the load her mother had gotten Elizabeth her own copy of that cookbook with the red checkered cover. That was how her love of cooking really got started.

When she first moved to Boston, she didn't know anyone and decided a good way to meet some people and incorporate a hobby was to take a few weekend cooking classes. This is how she met Robert and Jane. Robert is the owner/ instructor at the school and Jane was a fellow student in the class, a real estate lawyer during the week.

Over the course of a few classes, they became friends and made arrangements to meet outside the kitchen in various scenarios- dinner parties, hiking trips or wine tours, a couple ski trips to Sugarloaf or Mount Snow, shopping, here and there a concert or movie. Jane was able to help Elizabeth acquire her Beacon Hill row house apartment at a great price; Elizabeth helped both the school and Jane's firm to build a better business through effective advertising. Jane had even made several attempts to set Elizabeth up on dates, hoping that Elizabeth would find the same happiness that she had found in Robert. That's how Elizabeth came to meet Colin.

In the months and few years that followed their initial meeting, schedules became more erratic with their increasing work loads; occupational advancement tends to have that effect. The weeknight meet-ups and weekend trips became fewer and farther between and it was suggested that they create a small dinner co-op as a way to regularly share time and food. It'd been a great experience for all involved and had opened up a new avenue of business for Robert; in addition to their own small group on Saturdays, there was also a paying group that Robert's assistant oversaw on Sunday afternoons.

A couple glasses of wine and a few hours later, Elizabeth returned to her apartment carrying a canvas bag full of various meals portioned out and packaged in freezer/ microwave safe lidded containers, each meticulously labeled with contents and instructions.

Her own contribution of vegetarian lasagna was a well received success.

She went into her living area, which was really just a giant extension of her already spacious kitchen; the open floor plan one of the attractions she felt for the place. Sitting on the sofa with her feet propped up on the coffee table she unfurled the Boston Globe and opened the pages to the entertainment section looking for the movie listings.

Chapter 8

"It is my humble privilege to welcome you to our groundbreaking ceremony and celebration of the newest addition to the Atherton City landscape and to our community. On behalf of myself and the Atherton City Council, I would like to thank you all for joining us here today to witness and participate in this historic event." City Manager Diana Chavez-Arroyo stood at the podium and spoke over the wind. "I would first like to thank the city council, Parker Architectural and all the support staff involved in the long and arduous task of coordination and planning it took to get this project off the ground." She turned to several people sitting to her left and raised her hands in appreciative applause. When the cheering died down she continued, "There are a couple people here with us this evening, and one in particular," She glanced at Hailey and smiled. "Without whom this project wouldn't exist at all. It is because of her and her company's monumental generosity and desire to give back to the community that we have this land in the first place." This pronouncement was followed by polite cheers and applause. "In addition to the four acres of land that will comprise this park, Hailey Jensen and Jensen Industries Incorporated have given the city of Atherton the funding necessary to complete the project as envisioned, as well as the opportunity to create the new jobs that will come with the construction and maintenance of the space. It is with great pleasure that I welcome Hailey Jensen to the podium to say a few words before we commence with the celebration."

Hailey stood, smoothed the cream silk of her

slacks and slowly walked over to the podium. She took Diane's hand in hers and smiled her thanks as the flashbulbs went off. She had years of grooming for moments like these, but she still hoped her voice and bearing didn't betray her utter unease.

"Thank you Diane, and good afternoon to you." She turned to her audience, which was comprised mainly of city officials, family friends, friends of the company and those citizens who had some sort of financial or political interest in the goings on in their community. As one of the richest zip codes in the country, Atherton was not without more than its fair share of climbers and upstarts. Hailey gripped the podium and braced herself.

"When he was a young man just starting out, my father had a clear vision of what he wanted his life to be. More than anything else, he wanted to set a good example for everyone who might take notice, and this is something that he passed down to me." Her voice broke, and she took a couple seconds to steady herself. "Beyond accomplishing the successes he dreamed for his family and his business he wanted to give back to the community that he loved so dearly and he did so every chance he got, in ways both large and small – although many of his efforts you probably wouldn't recognize as his because in the true spirit of charity he didn't do these things to further his own name.

"He created a day of volunteering for his employees which allowed them two paid days a year to dedicate their time to any of the many charitable activities that occur here and in the surrounding communities. Over the years he donated millions of dollars to area charities, foundations, funds, organizations and hospitals to help ensure that the services and support they provide can continue. Just a few years before he died, he started the Fletcher Foundation, a non-profit organization dedicated to the memory of my brother and other kids who suffer severe brain damage through physical trauma. This is in addition to countless other acts of generosity that he committed throughout his life and is something that I and JII continue to do." She wiped at the tears threatening to fall and took a deep breath.

"'You cannot do a kindness too soon, because you never know how soon it will be too late.' This is something my father believed with all his heart, and it is his belief in this idea that propelled the Phillip Henry Jensen Memorial Park into becoming a reality. When he originally purchased this land it was to protect it from the sprawling development that was happening at the time and over the years he received several insanely lucrative offers from various interests to take it off his hands. But, he looked at it as an investment in the future. Now we can look at it as an investment in the community. I know that he would be proud of the effort going into making this a reality and I believe that the continued enjoyment of this space will honor his memory. Thank you and enjoy."

The crowd burst into cheers and applause, the flashbulbs strobed for several minutes while various parties shook hands and posed for photo-ops. When Hailey was finished with her speech, Peter wiped his own tears away, stood and wrapped an arm around her shoulder.

"You did great, Hails. He would be proud of you." He leaned in and placed a kiss on her temple.

~~~

"You look good enough to eat." Hailey felt the arms circle her waist from behind and her body stiffened at the sound of the too familiar voice. Hot breath touched her ear and she couldn't control the shiver it sent down her spine; the voice was much closer and dropped low for only her to hear. "If memory serves you taste good enough to eat, too."

Using her hands to pull out from the arms around her middle Hailey took a step away from Genevieve Warner's grip and turned to face her ex-lover. She hated to admit it, but Genevieve looked really good in her low cut silk halter and tailored black slacks that seemed to hug her curves in all the right spots. Once upon a time, Hailey would have given anything to trade places with those pants, but today it took a great effort of will to keep the venom from her voice and to not smack her where she stood. "Gen." She plastered a smile to her face that didn't come close to reaching her eyes. "I'd say it's a pleasant surprise to see you here, but it's neither of those things."

Feigning a hurt look she brought her hand to her chest and pouted. "Come on, don't be like that. We had some good times, didn't we?" She reached out and grabbed Hailey's arm, pulling her closer and pressing the length of their bodies together in a move that she knew at one time could make Hailey tremble with desire. Genevieve leaned in with her lips on Hailey's cheek. "I seem to remember some very good times. I can tell you still want me." Her voice was dripping with aspartame sweetness and Hailey cursed her body for its betrayal in responding. "Don't you miss it? I do."

"I might miss it if it had been any good, Gen."

She took a step away and looked her ex squarely in the eyes, standing only close enough to keep their conversation private. "Since we've been apart I've realized that I didn't love you. Hell, I didn't even like you, and if it weren't for the timing, I wouldn't even have known you left. You were just a way for me to keep from being bored, Gen. Surely you must know that by now." Gen dropped her hand from Hailey's body, the hurt in her eyes wasn't faked and for a second Hailey wondered if she'd gone too far.

"I know you don't mean that."

"You forfeited your right to know anything about me the day you walked away, Gen. How dare you come to me like this, in this place, on this of all days? Who the hell are you to think after everything you said and did at the end of us that I'd just welcome you back as if none of it happened?"

"Everything alright here?" Hailey didn't hear Peter walk up to them and was startled to hear his low voice as it broke her focus on Genevieve.

"Fine, Peter. I was just coming to find you." She gave him a relieved smile and looped her arm through his. "Have a nice life Gen. I hope you get everything you deserve."

Once they had moved several feet away, Hailey grabbed a Champaign flute from a tray passing by as Peter looked over his shoulder at Genevieve and asked, "What was that all about?"

"Just Gen being Gen and me finally putting her in her place."

"Wanna talk about it?"

"Nah, I'm good. Let's get out of here." She

downed her drink.

"Fine by me. Fosters?"

"You know me so well. I've been craving a twister like nobody's business."

They made the rounds to say their goodbyes and headed out to their favorite area ice cream shop.

Chapter 9

Sunday morning Elizabeth woke up in a tangle of sheets and limbs. The room was dark with very little light spilling through the blinds letting her know that it was well before dawn. She moved slowly, extracting herself from the bed, not wanting to wake up the slumbering body beside and half on top of her. It took a few moments for her eyes to adjust to being open and the darkness of the room as she tried to get her bearings, aware that she wasn't in her own bed; this never happens in her own bed. *Can't leave in the middle of the night and avoid the awkward 'well that was fun' morning after if it's your own damned bed.*

Once she was able to slide off onto the floor she stood and looked at the person whom she enjoyed the previous night. She took in the halo of blonde hair, the strong hands and long lean limbs, remembering all the sights and sounds and tastes and sensations as they used their entire bodies to explore every mound and dip of each other; a shiver travelled up her spine at the images.

Shaking herself free of the last vestiges of lassitude she turned to gather her clothing, following the trail out into the main living area. She was reminded of Hansel and Gretel and chuckled to herself at this, the juxtaposition of fairy tale innocence and the reality of her own debauchery.

In the bathroom, she dressed and examined herself in the mirror, noting the relaxed expression around her eyes, the still swollen lips, and the birds nest hair. Parts of her body were relaxed and limber, others spent and sore and knowing why made her smile.

Chapter 10

"Hey Patty- How's it going?" Hailey entered through the bakery's back door carrying a colorful gift bag that she held out to Patty. "I come bearing gifts," she said with a mischievous smile.

"Oh Honey, you know you don't have to do that," Patty said as she pulled Hailey into a warm hug. "How was your trip? Did you get everything done you needed to do?" Patty was covered in smears of cake batter and flour and various other baking ingredients. She swayed slightly on her feet and Hailey reached out an arm to steady her.

"Are you alright, Patty?" Her eyes widened with concern.

"Thanks. Just been feeling a bit dizzy today is all. I've been feeling a bit down for a couple weeks now." She shrugged. "I hope I'm not coming down with something, but I'd think if it was a bug I'd know by now."

"Maybe you ought to sit down for a few minutes; you're looking kind of pale." Hailey started to lead Patty back to her office where they could sit and chat out of the way for a few minutes. They didn't get two steps when Patty collapsed onto the floor.

"Patty! Oh my God. Patty!"

Chapter 11

"Good Morning, Jennifer. How was your weekend?" Elizabeth arrived at her office fifteen minutes past her usual time of 7:30, a box of fresh pastries and a paper coffee carrier balanced in one hand and her iPhone in the other as she was looking at the screen to see who was calling her; a number she didn't recognize.

"Good morning, Elizabeth. I had a low key weekend with Tom and his parents at their house on the cape. How about you? Did you do anything exciting?" She took the drink tray from Elizabeth and removed the coffees from the pressed paper holder. "Are these what I think they are?"

"Fruit tarts from your favorite little shop of pastry delights." She smiled warmly and waggled her eyebrows. "I had a pretty low-key weekend myself. I went to see that movie Hanna about the blonde girl that's raised by Eric Bana to assassinate Cate Blanchett. Have you seen it?"

Jennifer shook her head 'no.'

"It was pretty good. Interesting premise, and I love anything with Cate Blanchett; she's such a good actress."

"Yes, I love her too. Who's Eric Bana again?"

"He was in 'The Time Traveler's Wife.' That was such a good book."

"Oh yes, that's right. He also did that movie with Drew Barrymore about playing cards and falling in love…I forget the name of that one."

"Hmmm...I don't think I've seen that one. Oh well. Alright- what have we got going on today? Have we gotten many applications for the admin position?" Elizabeth picked up the stack of envelopes, files and messages that Jennifer handed her and started for her office, Jennifer following closely behind her with coffee and notebook in hand.

"We've gotten 17 applications for the position, 2 are internal, the rest have responded to the ad. I've already eliminated 5 based on their resumes and I'm on the fence about another. He lacks any real experience, but he finished with honors from Columbia with a degree in communications and a focus on design. I think that alone deserves at least an interview."

"He may be better suited for Wallace's team if he's any good with execution- with that kind of education he might be better served in the long run. Tate is going back to RISD to pursue his masters' and we'll need someone to fill that hole. Touch base with Wallace on this and find out if there's any interest, we might be able to get him in on that side of things, which is probably what this guy's aiming for in the long run anyway. Give the internal applicants priority – it would be nice not to have to train someone on our systems if we can help it."

They talked for another 5 or 6 minutes about the upcoming day, meetings, deadlines, emails that need responses, and so on. Jennifer was almost out of the office when she said, "Oh I almost forgot- there were several messages from a woman in Colorado- I didn't recognize her name...a Hailey Jensen? She left a call back number, but wouldn't elaborate further, just that it was urgent. Those and the rest of your messages are in the pile of mail I handed you earlier."

"Okay, Thanks Jennifer – Ah, here they are." She held up the small stack of pink message slips and waved them to Jennifer.

Hailey Jensen...that name isn't ringing any bells. From her desk phone, she dialed her mobile voice mail, listened to the automated menu and pressed one for new messages.

"Hi Elizabeth, I'm hoping this is the right number – if so, I've also tried reaching you at your office, but you must not be in yet. My name is Hailey Jensen, you don't know me but I'm a friend of your mother's. I don't want to cause a panic, but can you please call me as soon as you get this message? My cell number is (415) 555-5462." Elizabeth looked at her cell phone screen, pulling up missed calls and found that the call she ignored earlier was from the same number. *Of course.*

"Hi Elizabeth, this is Hailey again. Listen, I don't like to say this kind of stuff over the phone, but your mother's in the hospital- she's alright, but she needs you. Can you please give me a call as soon as you get this message so that I can give you more information? My number is (415) 555-5462."

The room was spinning and Elizabeth's stomach found its way to her throat as all the blood rushed from her head. All Elizabeth's life it had just been her and her mother. *This can't be happening. Please, God this can't be happening. Please let her be OK.*

She dialed the number Hailey had given her. "Jennifer?" She didn't usually holler for her assistant, but it's impossible to buzz a desk and make a call at the same time.

The panic in her voice must have been thick

because Jennifer came practically running. Elizabeth sat at her desk waiting for the call to go through, face pale, hands shaking, breath unsteady, and her eyes wide. Jennifer approached the desk, concern evident on her face. "Is everything alright?"

"Something's happened back home and I have to go remote for few days. I need you to open my schedule for the rest of the week and next week, and keep things to phone/ vid conference somewhat beyond that but only if it's necessary. Please let Harry know what's going on A.S.A.P.

"After that, I'll need you to send out an email to all my clients letting them know I'll be hard to reach for the next few days."

"This is Hailey." Elizabeth jumped at the sound of the voice coming through the receiver she held to her ear.

"Hi Hailey, this is Elizabeth Thornton returning your call- Can you hang on a second? I'm sorry." Elizabeth already had her hand cupping the mouthpiece.

"Sure, no problem."

She returned her attention to Jennifer, "Find out who on our team can handle them for now and then let the accounts know who to contact if it's urgent- ask Ellen and Joe P. first, they're senior…I'll need you to go into my schedule and make sure the processes that have to get started in the next few days happen and make sure that things continue to flow on target – looks like you can get an early start on that new position. Hand off what you need to hand off – Tony and Wallace both have light loads right now. As for the special accounts, put Katrina on the lead and if anyone gives any you grief about it, have them call me if they have a complaint. If you're not comfortable pushing all this out to the team, just set it up and I'll call an emergency staff meeting from the road and I can do it over the phone." Elizabeth looked to Jennifer for a reaction and Jennifer mouthed that she'd be fine to do it. Elizabeth nodded her acknowledgement and continued, "I need you to stay close for the next few minutes; I'll need you to book the soonest flight to Aspen they have, a car service to the airport from my apartment and possibly a rental once I arrive- I'll let you know the details shortly. Also- I'd appreciate it if you can contact HR and notify them of what's going on. You can have them email me whatever forms I need to fill out for this…OK I think that's it." She paused and made solid eye contact, "Thank you Jennifer."

"Don't worry, Elizabeth I'll take care of everything. I'm also making a note to contact IT so set your out of office messages. I'll put in a call to Mr. Gordon right now." With that, Jennifer exited Elizabeth's office and set about her tasks.

Elizabeth took a deep breath and tried to steady her shaking body. "Hello, Hailey? Thanks for waiting, I'm sorry about that…Yea, it's never a good time for this kind of thing- they'll live…Definitely. OK Tell me what I need to know."

Chapter 12

EquusAir flight 1527 from BOS to DEN took off with all the usual fanfare at 10:20am. According to Jennifer, Elizabeth could look forward to right around 10 hours of travel time including the one stop in Denver to switch planes to Aspen and then the drive from the airport to the hospital. She should get where she was going by 8pm by her body clock. Account for the time zones and that's right around dinner time in Colorado. *I don't know by what miracle Jennifer was able to book this flight on such short notice, but I need to get that woman a giant bouquet of flowers or something.*

Once they reached cruising altitude and the fasten seatbelt signs were turned off, Elizabeth turned her iPad on and started going through the emails she downloaded before take-off hoping to draft some responses to send out when they landed. *Anything is better than sitting here on this plane doing nothing but thinking about what might be wrong with my mom, even if I can't send anything off for another few hours.*

One of the best things about business class, besides the cushier seats is that you are much less likely to get chatted up the entire flight by someone who can't take a hint when your computer's on. True too is that there aren't any concerns that some kid is going to cry or kick your seat back the whole time. Just about everyone in this section has too much on their plate for frivolous interaction which suits her just fine. The more she could pour herself into her work, the less she had to think about why she was heading home.

Not that Hailey had given her much to go on, telling her that she'd much rather let Elizabeth's mother, Patty, fill her in once she gets there. All she knew was that her mom collapsed at work and is being kept for tests. Elizabeth could hardly recall a time when Patty was ever sick. To her knowledge, the only time her mom needed a doctor besides the regular annual exams was when she twisted her ankle on a patch of ice in their driveway. She probably would have skipped that visit too if it weren't for Elizabeth's insistence that she get it x-rayed because ankles aren't supposed to double in size and turn almost black purple. Luckily it was just a sprain.

All in all one could say they've been very lucky in this area, considering it wasn't until an introductory business course in college that Elizabeth learned what health insurance was. When she suggested that her mother get some and provide it to her staff as an added benefit, she found out just how hard it is for the average small business owner to afford such a luxury and what they could afford wasn't very comprehensive and had a very high deductible. A cafeteria plan they called it, but her mother did it because it was the best she could do and anything is better than nothing.

As a kid, Elizabeth didn't know the full extent of their finances- as most kids don't. She knew that there were some tight times when the clothes were patched to the point where they had become entirely different garments by virtue of extensive repair, or when she had to eat school lunches because they couldn't always afford to brown bag it. That she didn't have all the latest and greatest and her school supplies were often taken from the bakery office rather than getting the colorful notebooks and fuzzy pencils and whatnots the other kids had. That their car was old and beat up and backfired at the wrong times. But Patty did an excellent job stretching every penny and making sure that she and Elizabeth never hurt for lack of money. Everything that was necessity was covered as well as some small extras to keep them feeling special. Elizabeth never knew how many nights Patty stayed awake, especially in those early years, crying and trying to figure out how to make it all work, how to keep the house, how to get another year out of the car, how to get braces for her daughter.

She knew that her mother worked very hard to get her bakery business off the ground. Around the time Elizabeth turned two, Patty inherited a small fortune which she promptly put into the highest interest bearing savings account she could find and when Elizabeth entered 5th grade, Patty bought a rundown building in downtown Carbondale and spent every cent and minute she could turning it from an abandoned real estate office into a functioning bakery/café. She would start her day well before the sun leaving Elizabeth to ready herself for school and come to the bakery after to help with the after school rush and get things ready for the next day. More often Elizabeth would sit at one of the tables finishing her homework. "Someday, all of this is gonna to be yours Ellie-bean." Patty had told her, her face bright and full of pride for the fruits of their labors, a light dusting of flour in her hair, smudges of cookie dough or muffin batter or pie on her apron, an arm around Elizabeth's shoulder as they surveyed the now gleaming kitchen and dining area before they turned to head home for the night.

The bakery had started off simple serving coffee or tea, muffins, pies, cupcakes and cookies to the locals who soon became regulars. Over time she was able to hire some skilled staff and expand their offering to include soups, salads, breads and pastries which grew into sandwiches and some limited catering. Not including the cappuccino machine. Thanks to the newly booming tourist industry it's now a fairly bustling business with a staff of 15 and a rotating menu of over 50 items.

She understood that her mother had a heavy load of single handedly raising a daughter and starting a business and she worked very hard to make her mother's sacrifices worthwhile. This was part of the driving force behind her becoming her high school valedictorian and graduating summa cum laude before earning her MBA and going on to become upwardly mobile corporate dynamo she is today. At this last thought, she had to chuckle at herself. *Just wait 'til the 15 yr reunion later this year. Oh my God, is that this year?*

In Denver the overhead lights came on accompanied by that familiar "ding!" and the captain gave his 'thank you for choosing EquusAir welcome to Denver' spiel. She shook the stiffness out of her shoulders and neck from where she was sleeping with her face pressed against the window and activated the 3g on her iPad so she could send and receive emails while she was changing planes. After taxiing for what felt like an eternity the jet finally pulled up to the gate and the people emptied out.

After locating the screen bank she found her next flight and quickly made her way across the giant airport, making it to her gate just as the flight began to board. Forty-five more minutes in the air and she was coaching her breathing and body to relax and remain calm. If there's one thing that her mother had taught her, besides the idea that hard work is its own reward, it was that worrying about things before you know what they are doesn't do anyone any good. *Easier said than done this time, Mom.*

Chapter 13

Aspen/Pitkin County Airport was a small single runway serviced by 2 small airlines nestled in the majestic Rocky Mountains. It was one of those airports where you climb in and out of the plane from the ground rather than using a jet bridge at the gate. *MMMMM…Mountain air how I've missed you.* Elizabeth inhaled deeply and the crisp clean air filled her lungs and she immediately started feeling lighter. *I'm going to have to hold off on running for a few days until I get used to the altitude again.*

With the assistance of the service staff, she was able to get her bags and herself safely off the plane and onto the tarmac. Strapping her briefcase and bag to her luggage handle, she extended the grip and trucked it into the airport where a beautiful dark haired woman she didn't recognize was standing near one of the interior columns holding a sign that said "Thornton." She was dressed in jeans, a pea coat and scarf and a pair of buff colored knee high leather riding boots. When Elizabeth saw her she immediately noticed how tall the woman was, figuring her at just under her own height, and headed towards her. *How refreshing.*

As Elizabeth approached the woman, she put her at roughly the same age as herself, seeing that her eyes were a clear deep tone of blue and her long hair was not only dark but it was the rich brown of espresso. Combine these features with the rest of her face and this woman was movie star beautiful. Her face transformed into a warm smile of recognition and Elizabeth's breath caught in her throat, her stomach did a flip-flop. *Wow, this woman is absolutely gorgeous.*

The beautiful smiling woman extended her hand in greeting, a rich smooth voice saying, "You must be Elizabeth. I'm Hailey Jensen."

For a moment Elizabeth was dumb-struck but quickly recovered herself, shoving whatever thoughts she was having deep down into her mind and matching Hailey's smile with a tentative one of her own. "Yes. Hi Hailey, it's nice to finally meet you." She reached out and took Hailey's hand finding it soft and warm, the grip of her handshake firm but not in the competitive or over-compensating way that some people use. No, Hailey's handshake was confident and self assured, just as she hoped her own was.

"I've heard so much about you; your mother talks about you all the time. I'm just sorry we have to meet under these circumstances."

Elizabeth didn't know what to say as reply to this, only nodded her understanding, noting that she hadn't let go Hailey's hand. She loosed her grip and let her own hand find the pocket of her jacket, suddenly feeling awkwardly self conscious around this woman and not knowing exactly why.

If Hailey noticed Elizabeth's sudden unease, she didn't mention it. She bent to grab one of Elizabeth's bags, placed a hand on her shoulder and stepped aside indicating the exit with her free hand. "Shall we?" Her eyes were dancing with amusement and as Elizabeth proceeded to walk in front of her, she took the opportunity to get a good look at the long lean body, cocking her head to the side appreciatively to get a better view.

"Yes thank you, Hailey. I appreciate you coming all the way out here to pick me up. You certainly didn't have to do that."

"It's no trouble really. I enjoy the drive and it's nice to take a break from the hospital; your mom needs her rest anyway and there's only so much I can do," She said with a shrug.

As they reached Hailey's cherry red Jeep Wrangler Unlimited, Hailey clicked the keyless lock and opened the tailgate. She and Elizabeth put the bags in the back, and they set off on the hour long trip from Aspen to Mountain Crest Medical Center (MCMC) in Glenwood Springs.

"So Hailey, how do you know my mother?" The question sounded dubious even to her own ears, "I just mean to say, she hasn't mentioned you and I don't recognize you from around town." She recovered somewhat weakly.

Hailey chuckled light-heartedly at Elizabeth's stumbling line of questioning and glanced over to her, making eye contact to put her more at ease. "Well, there isn't all that much to tell, really. I moved to Carbondale some months ago from California and I met your mom at the bakery. I like to find a local hangout spot wherever I'm spending any significant amount of time and get to know the people there. I find that it's a great way to learn about the area and quickly become at least a small part of the community. After a couple weeks, Patty must have realized that I'm not just some adventure seeking tourist in town to tackle some trail or other and we started talking. She's a really easy person to talk to you know." She glanced at Elizabeth with a wink. For someone excruciatingly private, Patty had always been gregarious, which is probably part of why she's been so successful. Elizabeth looked out the window, but all her attention was on the woman sitting next to her.

"Anyway, when I broke my arm in a mountain biking accident a couple months after I arrived, she came by the house every day and brought sandwiches and goodies from the shop for me. When she went to visit you for Christmas I took in Riley so she wouldn't have to board him and checked in on the house to make sure the pipes hadn't burst or anything like that, shovel the walks, that kind of thing.

"She's really gone out of her way to make me feel like a welcome part of this place and I appreciate the hell out of her for it. I was visiting her at the bakery when she collapsed and I followed her in my car to the hospital. Of course, I did have to lie and tell the staff that I'm Patty's niece to be able to get in and see her." She chuckled, then Hailey placed her hand on the sleeve of Elizabeth's jacket for emphasis. "As far as I can tell, aside from the people on her staff and some familiar faces at the bakery or around town, you're the only other person she has in any kind of real way. I'm glad you were able to make it here on such short notice. She's really freaking out, even if she won't let it show."

Elizabeth was barely able to choke out a, "Thank you" before the tears started silently running down her cheeks. Suddenly hit with a tremendous feeling of guilt for living so far away and the ubiquitous fear of the unknown. "I'm just so scared; I wish I knew what's happening with her."

Chapter 14

Elizabeth left Hailey in the hallway and entered her mother's hospital room to find her lying in bed inundated with tubes and wires, surrounded by beeping machines. She didn't look all that sick, and anyone who didn't know her, didn't know the ever present rosiness to her cheeks or the smile that continually played at the corners of her mouth, might not suspect a thing. But Elizabeth recognized right away that her mother was not well. "Hey Mom," she said softly as she approached the bed.

"There's my beautiful Ellie-bean." Patty opened her eyes and stretched her arms out for a hug and Elizabeth gingerly gripped her mother and gently squeezed her shoulders before releasing her from the embrace and taking her hand in hers. She looked much smaller wrapped in the white hospital blankets; the bed swallowing her 5'7" frame making her appear more childlike, if not for the fine lines around her mouth and eyes and the streaks of white and silver scattered within her copper mane.

"How was your trip, Sweetheart?" Patty asked in an attempt at her usual cheery tone. It didn't go unnoticed by Elizabeth how thin her voice was or how miserably Patty had failed at sounding upbeat, the shimmering emerald of her eyes replaced by a dull olive a strong clue to the underlying state of illness.

Elizabeth couldn't help but let out a laugh, releasing some of the tension with it. "Jesus, Mom! If you wanted to get me home, you could have just asked." She squeezed her mom's hand lovingly and pulled up a chair to sit in.

"Elizabeth Marie Thornton – that is no way to talk to your dear old mother." Her amused tone belied the harshness of her words, and some of the glint had returned to her eyes.

Grateful for the small talk and the chance it provided to avoid the real issue, Elizabeth acquiesced. "The trip was fine, Mom. I can't believe Jennifer was able to get me a flight so quickly and with great seats too."

Patty pointed to the glass of water on the table that also held a mostly full dinner plate. Elizabeth handed it to her.

"But that's enough about me I'm worried about you Mom. What happened, have they told you anything?" Elizabeth was proud that she was able to keep the worry out of her voice.

"Nothing much yet; they're still waiting for some results. They've got me on fluids because they figure I'm dehydrated and apparently I'm anemic so they're pumping me full of vitamins and iron. They've been running all kinds of different tests- I've been poked, prodded, scanned, examined and practically interrogated. Now all we can do is to wait for the doctor to make up his mind as to what's wrong with me and let us know." She chuckled, handing the glass of water back to her daughter. "This must be why they call us patients."

While it warmed her heart to hear her mom making jokes, she had to groan at how corny it was.

"Knock, knock?" Hailey's voice softly called out and her head popped into the door. Patty waved her in, and she entered the room carrying a box from Organic Journey, one of the fancy new chain health food markets that have been popping up. "Hey," she said, waving to Patty. Turning to Elizabeth, "I didn't know how you take your coffee so I left it black but grabbed all the fixings. I also figured you must be hungry and had no idea what you would want, so I got a couple options." She poked around in the box and shuffled her feet a bit, looking tentatively between the two women before she continued. "I got a falafel wrap, a chicken salad sandwich, some chips...I know you're probably not hungry, but you should eat something." She placed the box on the table next to Elizabeth and went to stand on the other side of her near the foot of Patty's bed.

"Thank you, Hailey. That was very thoughtful of you." She tried not to sound surprised.

Patty smiled at the woman warmly. "Hailey has been a good friend; I'd have felt lost without her these last several hours."

Hailey blushed slightly and placed her hand on Patty's foot. Brushing the praise aside she looked at mother and daughter both, "Listen, I'm gonna let you get more caught up and head back home to check up on things and walk Riley." She turned to Elizabeth, "I've still got your bags in my Jeep – is there one you need me to bring in here for you or do you want me to just drop them at your mom's house?"

"Oh yes, I forgot all about my luggage." She made moves to get up but Hailey placed her hand on her shoulder and stopped her, "Honestly, I don't mind at all."

"Um...I guess if you don't mind you can just drop it off at Mom's. There's nothing that I'll need desperately before tomorrow." She had brought in the bag that held her necessaries. She could probably get a toothbrush in the gift shop and anything else could wait. "Thank you again."

Hailey squeezed her shoulder gently and let go reaching for Patty's foot and giving it a gentle squeeze too. "Ok then, ladies. I'll be back in the morning. If you need anything between now and then, you have my cell." With a smile and a wave she left the room.

"That Hailey's sure a dear. Interesting story too, but I'll let her tell you all about herself." Patty adjusted herself in the bed, pressing the button that raised the head into an even more seated position. "This hospital food is crap. Which one of these things do you want? I'm starving."

They ate in companionable silence for several minutes. Patty wasn't really all that hungry, but she knew she had to eat something and anything was better than the muck they tried to feed her earlier- mystery meat in brown gravy, soupy mashed potatoes, soggy steamed vegetables and green Jell-o. Patty screwed her face up in disgust as she thought about it.

As Elizabeth was gathering the last of the food evidence there came a light knock on the door followed promptly by a short, thin, gray haired man wearing a white coat and stethoscope in addition to a blue button down, khaki trousers and black sneakers. His expression gave away nothing as he entered the room; he greeted them both by shaking their hands and addressed his patient.

"Hello Patty, I'm Dr. Jeremy Martin. I'm the Chief of Oncology here at Mountain Crest Medical Center. I'm sorry you had to wait so long to get news from us as to the status of your condition. When we deliver any kind of news, we like to be absolutely certain that it's correct, hence all the testing and waiting." *Did he say 'Oncology?'* Nodding to himself as if reconfirming the findings, he looked Patty in the eye. "Patty, there's no easy way to tell you this, so I'm just going to say it. The bad news is that you have cancer. Specifically, it's called…"

Elizabeth stopped hearing what Dr. Martin was saying; she didn't mean to, but the shock of the news was too much to take. She felt as if the bottom of the world dropped away. She watched the doctor's lips moving, looked to her mother's hand gripped in her own, raised her eyes to look at her mother's face. Patty looked just as stunned, whatever color had been there was now completely drained and her eyes were glassy. *Get it together Elizabeth. You can't fall apart now, and you absolutely cannot fall apart in front of your mother. She needs you more than she's ever needed you and you have to pull yourself the fuck together!* She straightened her spine and tried to focus on hearing the doctor's words.

"…some success with this two pronged approach to treatment, although I have to tell you it's going to be a long and hard road ahead. I'd like for us to get started on this as soon as you've recovered from yesterday's episode and have had a few days to make whatever arrangements you need. Your fluids and iron levels should be getting back up to where we need them at the end of this bag and after some decent rest tonight you should be ready by tomorrow to get the line implanted and start treatment in a couple days if everything tests well. The sooner we get going, the sooner we'll start to see results.

"Now as with any cancer treatments, there are risks and side effects. I've brought some pamphlets and information for you to read through. You should make whatever arrangements you need to over the next couple days, since I doubt you'll want to do much once the treatments start." He paused and turned squarely back to address the room. "I know this is a lot to take in. This is shocking news and it's hard to hear. I'll leave you to process all this and get some rest. I'll be back by in the morning to talk more at length with you about it and answer whatever questions you may have."

Dr. Martin looked into the faces of the women he was talking to. He saw their fear and sorrow and uncertainty and shock. This was a look he had seen all too often on too many faces in his line of work and it never got any easier. Medical school and years of experience had taught him that getting attached or emotionally involved would eventually eat him alive, and he tried always to remain as detached as possible, but how do you maintain humanity that way? It's impossible to be a good doctor dealing with sick people every day, good people, and sometimes for months on end, to not have some investment in their care and provide for them the care and compassion they need. This wasn't just a job to him, some way to get great money and have nice things and respect in the community. No, for Dr. Jeremy Martin, this was a calling to a higher purpose, decided for him the day his little brother died of leukemia when they were kids.

Elizabeth squeezed Patty's hand and looked at her mother, who returned her gaze but didn't really see. She knew better than to ask Dr. Martin if her mother would be ok. There was nothing ok about this, and nothing would ever be the same.

"We'll get through this, Mom. I'm here, I'm not going anywhere. We'll get through this together."

~~~

Some time later that first night, after Patty had drifted off to sleep, Elizabeth was sitting in the hospital's chapel utterly and completely stunned. There was no comfort to be had in the worn-smooth wood of the pews, in the warm rich colors of the carpet or drapes meant to feel like a hug, in the calming soft light or in the scent of the candles burning. The images of Mary and the various saints not invoking the feelings of safety, piety and awe that they once did when she was a kid; instead, their carved faces held only empty eyes and uncaring expressions.

Cancer. Fucking cancer?! And she knew it had to be serious when they did the lumbar puncture - she knew! Why didn't she tell me? Ok, let's be reasonable, Elle- why would she tell you something like that without conclusive proof? It had already happened; you couldn't do anything about it anyway. You know Mom doesn't like to cause unnecessary worry. Did Hailey know?

What did the doctor say? Acute Myo-something-or-other. What did the doctor say? Why did I zone out? The most important news you'll probably ever get and you can't even keep it together long enough to hear all of it? Twenty to forty percent chance of survival? Oh my God, I don't know if I can deal with this. If you're there, God, please help me to be strong. I know I haven't talked to you much in recent years, but I need you now. Please let her be OK.

Chapter 15

"Hey there beautiful; I was just in the- oh."

Hailey was wrapped in a towel from swimming. She had been crying when Zoë DioCosta's five foot six inches bounced around the corner of the house to find her sitting on the edge of one of her patio chairs with her shoulders slumped, her head down. She looked up at the welcome voice of her friend and gave a small smile of greeting.

"Hey."

Zoë offered her hand to Hailey, "C'mon let's get you inside- don't you know it's freezing out here?"

Hailey had been so caught up that she didn't realize she was shivering. She took Zoë's hand and got to her feet, wrapping the towel tighter around her shoulders. Zoë reached up and wiped the tears from Hailey's cheeks, brushed the hair out of her face and stood on her tip toes to kiss her lightly on the lips before pulling her into a tight hug. Hailey's body sagged into the embrace and she began to sob again.

Zoë stroked her hair and whispered reassurances to her. "Shhh. Honey, it's ok. It'll be OK. Let's go inside and you can tell me all about it ok?" Hailey only nodded and shuffled along behind her.

"Here let's get you warmed up. You wait right here while I get the fire going and then we'll have a hot shower and I'll blow dry your hair and take care of you tonight." She tilted Hailey's chin so that their eyes met. "Sound like a plan?"

Hailey only nodded, still appearing shell shocked.

Zoë removed her shoes by the back door and left Hailey standing in the kitchen to take the few steps into the living room where the remote for the gas fireplace and the central heating controls lived. A few seconds later, a fire roared to life in the hearth and a warmer temperature was entered into the thermostat.

Zoë led Hailey to the back of the house where the master bedroom and bath were located. She opened the glass shower door and expertly navigated the large multi head shower system so that several of the heads were spouting a gentle stream of soon to be hot water. Moving slowly, she murmured comforting sounds to Hailey as she took the large towel from her and tossed it away, then ushered Hailey into the now steaming cascade. A few moments later, she stepped naked into the spray wrapping her arms around Hailey and holding her fast in the water.

Hailey held onto Zoë like a woman drowning. Her sobs were quiet, marked only by the shaking of her shoulders and the shaky catch of her breath into Zoë's hair.

"Talk to me, Honey. Tell me what's got you so upset."

"It's just like my Nonna all over again. I don't know what I'll do if I lose her too."

"Lose who, Honey?"

"Patty. My friend Patty just got diagnosed with the same Leukemia that my Nonna died from."

"Oh Baby, I'm so sorry." She hugged her tighter and kissed her cheek. "Listen to me, okay? Your Nonna died what? Fifteen years ago, right?" A nod. "They've made a lot of medical advancements in fifteen years, right?" Another nod. "People survive cancer all

66

the time nowadays, more and more." She pulled back from Hailey to look her in the eyes. "You have to believe that. Patty needs you to believe that right now."

"I want to believe that, Zoë – you know I do, and in my head I know you're right. But it just brings up every fear and worry and pain I have. I'm so scared for her."

They stood under the water until the stream turned tepid, until Hailey's sobs ceased. "I don't want to be alone tonight."

"Don't worry, Sweetie. I'm not going anywhere. We've got all the time in the world. I'm going to help you forget for a while."

Chapter 16

Two days after getting the news, Elizabeth and Patty were quietly sitting in the sunroom sipping tea and watching the squirrels competing for the fallen seeds from the birdfeeder as well as the occasional cardinal, towhee or jay. When Elizabeth was a kid, when this room was still an open patio, they would sit under the summer shade for entire afternoons counting and naming the different birds that would come into view: swifts, swallows, phoebes, flycatchers, nutcrackers, buntings, grosbeaks, finches, robins, sparrows and so on. The frenzied flutter of hummingbirds visiting the feeders or any number of the various climbing and ground flowers that Patty added to the landscape over the years; Honeysuckles, roses, morning glories, bee balm, cannas, lilies, columbines, and various other wild flowers.

Patty never was one to watch a lot of TV instead spending her time tending to and enjoying her home when she wasn't working at the bakery. Over the years she had created quite a paradise for herself and the plants and animals that lived there. At dawn and dusk even the occasional rabbit, deer or fox might be glimpsed and even rarer sometimes a bobcat, perhaps skirting the edge of its hunting area or searching for easier food in leaner months. Such were the benefits of living a bit away from town. A fifteen or twenty minute drive will give you all the conveniences of the modern world but you get to keep the natural world at your backdoor.

The silence between mother and daughter was companionable if not comfortable, both content for the moment to ignore the elephant in the room and simply soak up the remains of the day. The major decisions had been made for now, the arrangements and preparations all settled and nothing to do for the moment but to wait for the morning when Patty's chemo treatments began. Elizabeth was holding Patty's hand in her lap, a gesture that provided comfort to them both.

A gentle knock on the door and Riley's subsequent barking broke through Elizabeth's reverie. "I'll get it, Mom. Can I get you anything while I'm up?"

"Maybe just a glass of water Dear, thank you." Patty handed Elizabeth her empty tea cup and returned her gaze to the large picture window.

Elizabeth carried their empty cups through the house to the door, battling for a spot against the overzealous Irish setter who was fiercely wagging his tail and pawing at the door.

"Riley that's enough. Go sit you crazy goof ball." Through the stained glass pane in the front door Elizabeth could make out the shape of Hailey. She opened the door to beautiful azure eyes smiling back at her. Hailey's hair was tied back into a simple loose knot, her jeans and pink long sleeved Henley hugging all the right spots and Elizabeth's heart fluttered at the sight.

"Hi."

"Hailey! Hi. Come on in. Riley get down!" She reached her free hand out and grabbed Riley by the collar as he was trying to knock Hailey down in the doorway to get a better angle on licking her face off. "I'll just take him out to his run and let him burn some of this off – Mom's out in the sunroom."

"I brought some dinner, wine and a few games –

I hope you don't mind." Hailey followed Elizabeth and Riley through to the kitchen and placed her bags on the counter and started to empty them while Elizabeth put Riley out into his own yard. "Patty and I have been sharing a meal and entertainment every Wednesday evening for a while now and I thought it might be good to keep that routine- you know, maintain some semblance of normalcy. Plus it might be a nice distraction. If you don't agree, I can just go visit with her for a spell and then leave you with it...if that's what you prefer..." For some reason, Hailey was suddenly unsure of herself for seemingly barging in. If Elizabeth noticed, she didn't show it.

"I think that's a great idea Hailey and I know Mom will appreciate the company. I'm glad she has a friend in you." Elizabeth placed the empty teacups into the dishwasher and was getting some ice water for Patty. "Can I get you something to drink?"

"Oh no, I have my Sigg." She held up her stylish steel water bottle by way of explanation. "Thank you though." She reached out and placed her hand on Elizabeth's arm, "You know...you have a friend in me too. I've mostly stayed away these past couple days to let you both adjust to what's happening, but I'm here to help if you'll let me." The sincerity of the statement was conveyed in her voice, the concern written in her eyes and while Elizabeth generally felt herself to be independent and capable, she knew this was going to be something she could not do on her own.

"Thank you, Hailey. I appreciate that," she said seriously then added lightly in an attempt at levity, "I'm sure we'll need it so I hope you don't live to regret the offer."

"I wondered where you'd gone off too," Patty said as she entered the kitchen. "Why didn't you tell me Hailey was here?" She said, reaching arms out to give Hailey a hug of greeting, something she reserved only for Elizabeth and a few close friends over the years. Elizabeth was warmed by the light returned to her mother's eyes as the pleasure of seeing Hailey registered there. For a few brief moments at least, the heaviness of the last couple days was lifted by the simple joy of a friend.

"I've brought your favorite," Hailey said to Patty. "Fontina stuffed chicken breasts wrapped in prosciutto with mushrooms, asparagus and linguini in a nice lemon beurre blanc, garlic bread and some pinot grigio. Everything I need is here." She patted the canvas bag with various Tupperware and baking dishes with a smile. "Just have to cook it up whenever we're ready – shouldn't take more than twenty minutes."

Elizabeth's eyes are wide and her eyebrows are raised in surprise as she looked from behind Hailey to her mother who was smiling back and forth between her and Hailey. "Wow that sounds wonderful. You didn't have to go through all that trouble, Hailey."

"Oh it's really no bother." She replied in earnest. "Like I've told your mom, it's just as easy to cook for a few as it is to cook for one and I have to eat too so it's not a big deal. Besides, eating with friends beats eating alone any day and like my Nonna used to say, 'no better way to show you care than with good food.'" For the briefest second a dark cloud washed over Hailey's face, but she quickly recovered and tossed a wink to Patty. "Besides, cooking it up is part of the entertainment."

"Well it sounds wonderful, Hailey. Why don't

we store this stuff for a little bit later and you can come out to the sunroom and let us know what's been happening with you these past couple days." Patty opened the fridge to make room for Hailey's parcels and Elizabeth went to get Riley back into the house while Hailey emptied the rest of the food items from her sack.

A few minutes later they were all gathered in the sunroom sitting in the various seats, Riley with his butt on the floor and paws on Hailey's knees reveling in the vigorous attention that she was giving him.

"So Patty tells me that you work at an advertising firm in Boston?"

"She's the youngest Senior Vice President in the history of the firm." Patty beamed at her daughter with pride. "And the only female on the executive team- she's even on their website!"

Hailey arched an eyebrow and Elizabeth chuckled lightly, feeling both pleased and bashful at the praise. The high walls of protection she'd built around herself over the years easily shattered by her mom and being back home. "Well, that's true enough Mom- although we do have several female directors and managers that will be candidates for executive positions as the company grows and positions become available." Turning to address her mother directly, "As a matter of fact, did I tell you that I created a new position for Jennifer that puts her in line for VP in a few years?"

"No, I don't think you've mentioned that yet Ellie. I bet she was surprised and pleased- how did you manage it?"

To Hailey she explains, "Jennifer was my Assistant." Hailey nods in understanding. "I created the position of Strategic Accounts Manager which puts her on track for a director position, and eventually my job if she's inclined.   She'll be coordinating between the various teams and departments to ensure that campaigns don't get snagged up in the quagmire of process, setting priorities based on schedules and client expectation, troubleshooting, etc.   It's actually a big relief for me, since it takes some of my workload which will let me focus more on bringing in new accounts and it's pretty much what she's been doing the last few months anyway minus the more mundane aspects like making coffee and copies." *Am I babbling? Why am I babbling?*

"Wow," Hailey said. "That's quite a transition from assistant to management, she must have been excited."

"Well, I'm a firm believer in rewarding hard work and talent," she looked fondly to her mother, acknowledging the hard work that her mother has done her entire life and the value that was passed between them. "And Jennifer has both in spades. I knew when I hired her that it would be a transitory deal; she graduated in the top 10 at BC, came highly recommended via prestigious internships and has been the best EA I've ever had- for me it was a no brainer. At least this way we'll be utilizing all of her talents and not just her well honed organizational skills." At this she chuckled and reached for her drink.

"That's wonderful, Ellie. I know from what you've told me over the past couple years or so that she's been a huge asset." The pride she had in her daughter's action was obvious in the dancing eyes and warm smile she gave her and Elizabeth returned the expression with a grin of her own. "That's enough

73

about me. What do you do for work, Hailey?"

Hailey cleared her throat and glanced at Patty quickly then said, "I'm a sculptor."

"A sculptor? That's cool – what kind of pieces do you create? Would I have seen any of it?" Elizabeth leaned forward to place her glass on the coffee table and remained to give Hailey her full attention.

"Well, I do a lot of architectural sculpture and installations, mainly for the corporate market, but I do have a few pieces in private collections." She took a sip from her Sigg and shifted her position in the chair. "I'm currently working on a commission for my hometown, a 12'x20'x7' bronze abstract of the sea that will be installed in one of the parks near the bay. That should be completed in late May/ early June – provided the process doesn't get 'snagged in the quagmire of process' to borrow your phrase." When Hailey spoke of her art it was clear that this was a passion for her. She was animated and spoke with her hands, her whole face alight with the barely bridled excitement she felt for her occupation. Elizabeth was enthralled watching her.

"When creating a bronze, there are a few bits of the process that I outsource to one of the foundries I utilize. This piece will be forged in Oregon and trucked down to the park for delivery. I create the positive in plaster or plywood or whatever medium lends itself best to the form – sometimes I use wire and screen, sometimes papier-mâché...it really depends on the piece...large ones like this I might even use a 3d rendering software to translate a smaller model up to scale. This is really great for modeling and helps to determine whether the piece will be structurally sound. Then I provide the specifications and if necessary go to the forge itself and oversee the finishing process – although the forges I use these days pretty much know what I want and I trust them."

"Wow, that's really amazing, Hailey. I would love to see some of your work sometime."

"Elizabeth got her initial degree in Fine Art before getting her Master's in Business. You have something in common. In fact, many of the paintings hanging up around the house are hers." At this, Hailey merely raised her eyebrows and looked at Elizabeth more appreciatively, not wanting to interrupt the flow of conversation as Elizabeth had already begun to speak.

"Well, actually it was a BFA-AH. The studio arts practicum was a challenging and an awesome experience that I've been able to use in my career but the history is really what I found most fascinating. I'm really quite a nerd at heart."

"Yes, I agree to some extent, although my own studies were somewhat divergent as well, which didn't give me much of a chance to study as much of the history as I would have liked. I got my BFA at RISD and a simultaneous BSA through Brown where I went on to complete a masters in their PRIME program per my fathers insistence." Her expression clouded for a second, so quickly that Elizabeth wasn't sure she'd seen it. "I've since gone back and got my MFA through UCLA." With this statement Hailey shook her Sigg indicating its empty status. "My water is empty- are you guys ready to start dinner?"

Elizabeth's own stomach chose that time to grumble its loud assent and everyone burst into laughter. "Yes it would seem it's about that time! Come on girls, we can continue this conversation in the kitchen." Patty rose from her seat and gathered her own empty water glass from the side table. "You girls are both so accomplished it's almost like I'm sitting in on an over-achievers anonymous meeting." Her tone was teasing and she poked Elizabeth playfully in the side. Elizabeth giggled at this and wrapped an arm around her mother's shoulders as they walked together to the kitchen.

"I don't know about that, Patty- I think with all you've done so far you could be the president of that little club." Patty flashed her 'yea right' expression at Hailey.

"Seriously, single handedly raising a child into a successful adult while completing a degree going part time at night and also founding a successful business from scratch? Come on, that's some really heavy accomplishment. Many women in your position only marginally succeed at one of those goals, let alone all three. That takes a special kind of strength and determination Patty and it's truly inspiring; I am in awe. It's obvious where Elizabeth gets her drive from."

Patty smiled at the praise and a blush was creeping up her neck so unused to candid positive appraisal was she. "Oh now, cut that out, you. My head's gonna get so big I won't be able to get it through the door." Hailey giggled in response.

"Truly though, Mom you know I agree with Hailey. It's still hard for women today and we don't have to face nearly the social and economic obstacles you had to overcome. There are more and more opportunities for women to get scholarships, business loans and other aid and resources to help insure our success if we need it and it's still hard. Don't short sell yourself, you're amazing."

"Ah well. You know," She brushed a stray tear from her cheek and stood from her stool, wrapped her arms around her daughter and kissed the top of her head, "my best achievement will always be you, Ellie-bean."

Elizabeth returned the hug with a tight grip and Hailey turned her attention to filling a pot with water to boil the pasta in. "I love you too, Mom. We'll get through this too," she whispered, releasing Patty from the hug to wipe at her own eyes. "I'm going to let Riley out. Do you want to hear some music?"

"That sounds like a great idea, Ellie."

"Any requests?"

"I'm easy."

"Me too, Sweetie – you know what I like. Is there anything I can do to help, Hailey?"

"You just sit there and look beautiful – we'll take care of the rest, won't we Elizabeth?" Hailey had all the ingredients out of the fridge and a skillet was already heating up.

"You bet- don't worry about this Mom, we've got it. You just relax. Come on, Riley."

Lord give me the strength.

After a few moments outside gathering herself back up, she re-entered the kitchen and placed her iPod into the Bose sound system that she gave Patty for Christmas last year and softly played an eclectic all female playlist.

"Oh my God I love this song!" Hailey exclaimed

when LP's 'Into the Wild' came on. "So, Elizabeth, did you always want to be in advertising?"

She laughed lightly, "Oh no. I wanted to be a ballerina, but by 11 I was already way too tall and my growth spurts had thrown my coordination all out of whack anyway so I moved on to different dreams before I realized you can't eat dreams and they don't pay the rent," She said with a shrug, her voice tinged with sadness. She shook it off and changed the subject, "Damn that smells good, what can I do to help?" *Why am I telling her all this stuff? She doesn't need to know how awkward I was as a kid!*

"We're just about done actually- just need to pop the loaf of garlic bread into the broiler in a few minutes and get that toasted and it's done. I did all the prep at home, so all I had to do really was pop stuff into the heat and let it do its thing. Oh- the wine!" She snapped her fingers, opened the fridge and pulled a chilled bottle of pinot grigio from the door. "This needs to be opened and poured if you want." She reached out the bottle for Elizabeth who took it willingly and reached around Hailey to open the drawer where the corkscrew lived. They moved around the room as if in a well choreographed dance, Hailey putting the finishing touches on dinner and Elizabeth getting the dishes, glasses and flatware. *I can't remember a time ever besides with Mom when it was this easy to just be in a kitchen with someone.*

"I'll set the table and put the wineglasses out there. Mom- do you want me to refill your water?"

"Sure, Honey- thanks. I'll go let Riley in and make sure he gets his dinner."

A little while later they were all sitting around the table, their plates all nearly empty and pushed away and each with a satisfied food-glow and smiles on their faces. The conversation had been easy, the meal was delicious and Elizabeth could definitely see why her mother would be taken with this gorgeous young woman named Hailey Jensen. She perceived an easy going, genuine and warm hearted soul there, a refreshing candor and wit, wonderful sense of humor and a disarming blitheness in her demeanor that belied a general seriousness and made it very easy for Elizabeth to open up and speak candidly with this virtual stranger about things she rarely told anyone- not even Jane and Rob. *What is it about this woman that makes me feel safe enough to just open up like that? Is it because of my mom and everything going on there? Am I just raw? Does it matter?*

"Who wants dessert?" Hailey asked as she was reaching for Patty and Elizabeth's empty plates stacking them on her own and rising to take them to the kitchen.

"You didn't." Patty's eyes were wide and although she was filled to the brim, she couldn't stifle her excitement for what she hoped was coming next.

"Indeed I did." She replied with a mischievous glint in her eyes. "Elizabeth, can I get a hand?"

"Sure- be right there. Mom- you want anything? A refill?"

"Actually, I'll take a small glass of rice milk if you don't mind." Elizabeth leaned over to get Patty's empty water and wine glasses and kissed the top of her head.

"No problem."

When she entered the kitchen she found Hailey taking the lid off a glass baking dish filled with the mystery dessert. "Whatcha got there?" She asked as she poked her head over Hailey's shoulder to get a better look.

"This is my Nonna's secret family recipe tiramisu. It's one of Patty's favorites and I figured in light of everything, a decadent treat would be a good thing."

"You didn't have to go through all this trouble, but I know it's very appreciated- by us both. Thank you."

"You don't have to thank me. Like I said before, I'm here to help. Patty has been a Godsend to me since I moved here and I know that after tomorrow food is likely to be an entirely unenjoyable experience for a while." Her eyes were kind with a hint of sadness around the corners when she looked into Elizabeth's. "Ok – all plated up! Nice idea with the tray, by the way – and thanks for the glass of 'milk.'"

Later that night, Elizabeth was lying awake in her bed, listening to the sounds of the house and the wind outside. Riley's head was on her belly and she was absentmindedly scratching his ears. The afternoon was wonderful. For a few hours they were able to forget the heaviness of what was about to happen and simply enjoy good food, a new friend and each other. Stories came easily and they had laughed several times, a sound that had been painfully absent in the time since learning about the cancer. But now Hailey had gone home, Patty retired to her own room and the clock was ticking away the wee hours while Elizabeth fought against the building tightness in her chest and the sense of impending doom. *Now's not the time for this Elizabeth. We need to remain optimistic…there's a fighting chance and we're gonna take it!*

Chapter 17

Modern architecture, walls of glass and beige tile welcomed Patty and Elizabeth to the Kathleen Roark Wing of the MCMC, where the cancer center was located. Following the signs, a rose colored paint stripe on the wall led them into the treatment area where they registered, waited for Patty's name to be called and then were led through the large double doors by a tech into the treatment area, stopping off first to get weighed and to have some blood drawn.

A middle aged woman dressed in pink scrubs with kind eyes, salt and pepper hair and a slightly ruddy complexion took the file from the tech and ushered them to a sitting area comprised of several beige chairs that looked like a cross between dentist chairs and recliners.

"Hi Patty, I'm June. You must be Elizabeth," She said to them in turn and shook their hands. "I'll be overseeing your treatment today- if you have any questions or need anything just let me know. How are you feeling this morning?"

"Nervous. Scared. Uncertain. Optimistic." Patty chuckled to lighten the mood and it came out a bit shaky. Elizabeth put her arm around her mother's shoulder and gave her a light squeeze.

"That's perfectly understandable and natural Patty; just know that I and the rest of my team are here for you and we're going to do everything we can to get you through this. Why don't you have a seat here," she indicated one of the large beige loungers. "Elizabeth you can sit here if you'd like." Indicating the lounger directly adjacent, "Most days we have at least one free seat among these and I'll be sure to put you where you can use both if you'd like. I know Dr. Martin has filled you in on this process but I'll just remind you now and then if you have questions along the way I'll gladly address them for you." As she was talking she laid everything out that she'd need to get things going.

"As you know, Dr. Martin implanted a Port-a-Cath into your chest on Tuesday morning. That is how we will be delivering your meds to you. Today we will be starting your Remission Induction Chemo round-that's the first phase of your therapy and will consist of 7 consecutive days of treatment, each session lasting around 5 hours. The first 3 days you will receive 2 types of chemo drugs in addition to a few other drugs that will help you with comfort and well—being and then one of the chemo drugs will be removed on day four for the remainder of the course."

"What can we expect during all this?" Elizabeth asked. Her face drained of its color as was Patty's.

"Well, that's a good question. First I'll need to examine the site of your port and make sure the skin is adequately healed and healthy then I'll disinfect the area, apply a topical anesthetic to reduce the pain and inject some saline to flush the line. Once that's finished, I'll attach the bag and let it flow. As you receive the meds, you'll probably feel any combination of sensations including a spreading chill, perhaps slight burning or tingling and general strangeness. You may feel tired, maybe a bit of fever or chills, a little nauseous–although there will be Zofran and a few other things to help with that.

"You may not feel much of that at all- it really

depends on how your body handles it. Other side effects may present themselves when you get home. I'll give you some materials on it that will let you know exactly which drugs you're getting, what dosage, what the side effects might be, etc. You'll want to get home and stay home until you understand how your body processes the drugs and later if you have to leave, you will need to wear a mask. As you know, chemotherapy doesn't distinguish between cancer cells and normal cells, so your immune system is going to take a huge hit. Usually this treatment is done in hospital where we can control the environment, but you live nearby and have someone looking out for you so you should be OK.

"You're also very likely to feel weak and quite ill. We'll be sending you home with an antiemetic as well as anti-nausea medication to help curb that feeling, but it may not be 100% effective for you. You'll want to stay well hydrated and I recommend a neutral flavored Gatorade or plain Pedialyte to help keep your salts up. If the vomiting persists, you'll want to stop eating until it stops and then slowly reintroduce bland foods as the feeling subsides. Keep us informed of all of this, and if you're unable to take in food we'll provide nutrition through the port."

"Jesus. This sounds like the most fun I'll ever have! Let's get started right now." Patty straightened her shoulders and steeled herself and when Elizabeth grabbed her hand, she squeezed it back and said, "It'll be ok, Ellie. I'll be ok. They're gonna take care of it, right June?"

She fixed them each with solid eye contact in turn. "I can promise you this: we're going to do everything we can."

Chapter 18

"You sound better today."

"Yea, I spent the evening over at Patty's like we do every Wednesday and it was pretty awesome. I really should be thanking you though. I'm sorry I cracked up on you like that." Hailey was talking into her wireless earpiece, driving her jeep along the famous West Elk Loop, a 205 mile stretch of road that wound its way around mountains lakes and rivers providing a nice day drive filled with scenic vistas and plenty of options for getting out of the car. It was a good excuse to get out of the house and do something mindless.

"Oh, Hailey that's what friends are for- you don't have to thank me. We've known each other what? 10 years? 11? I'm pretty sure even if I didn't love you dearly that I probably owe you some shoulder time, so lay it on me Baby- my back's strong. Speaking of backs," she added in a suggestive tone, "it's not like it was all tears. For a few hours before sleep took us I rather enjoyed myself and I'm fairly certain that you did as well."

"Like I said, I should be thanking you. By the way, how's it going with Cindy?"

"Ugh. Don't ask. Well I would have mentioned it the other night, but it didn't seem relevant. She wanted me to move in with her, but it didn't feel right, you know? I mean, we've only been dating for a couple months and it's not like we were exclusive or even that serious…So when I hesitated she took it as a complete rejection and went completely bat-shit on me. Now I can't get her to stop calling me."

"Wow. So she must be who that cliché is based on. And you were honest with her from the beginning?"

"What? You mean about keeping it casual and seeing where it goes? Of course! I'm nothing if not upfront. Anyway, I'm seeing Jesse again tonight. This will be our 3rd date and you know what that means."

Hailey laughed. "You are such a dog. If I didn't have my own proof I might mistake you for a guy. Is Jesse the hair dresser or the horse whisperer or is she one you forgot to mention?"

"She raises and trains show horses for your information, and don't judge; you weren't complaining about my sexual activity the other night. So let's turn the tables – when are you going to find someone for yourself?" Unbidden flashes of Elizabeth's face flared up in Hailey's mind causing her breath to catch and cough. "I'd set you up with one of my friends, but I'm selfish and you don't want the ones I've weeded out anyway."

"Yea- your sloppy seconds are not on my menu at all. Right now I'm happy with the status quo. You're the one who seems to have a problem with the fact that I haven't partnered, and might I remind *you* that that wasn't a problem the other night." *Not to mention the fact that there might be someone I'm interested in, but it's way too early to talk about it. It's complicated. Too complicated, I shouldn't even be thinking about it, in fact.*

Chapter 19

"Oh God, I have to do this again tomorrow?" Patty was sitting on the bathroom floor, Elizabeth had put her hair into a loose ponytail to keep it out of her face and with a hand on her shoulder she handed her mother a paper towel to wipe her mouth followed by a glass of water to rinse with. It was 7pm and they'd been home since around 2, and despite the antiemetic and anti-nausea medication the hospital provided, the last couple hours have been spent either in or very nearby the bathroom while Patty lost every ounce of whatever could possibly left in her stomach and then some.

"Why don't we get you into bed, Mom…I'll bring in a trashcan for you and maybe you can get some rest."

"Yea, that sounds like a good plan."

Elizabeth helped Patty up from the floor, grabbed the trashcan from under the sink and led Patty to her bedroom.

"I'll let you get dressed in something more appropriate, Mom. Just put what you're wearing into your hamper and I'll put it in with my stuff to do a load tonight. I'm going to get you some crackers and Gatorade for when your stomach is settled a bit – be right back."

Several minutes later, Elizabeth returned to Patty's room to find her dressed in her pajamas and sleeping in her bed. She placed the items she brought on the bedside table and slowly backed out of the room, dragging the laundry with her.

In the kitchen she booted up her laptop and was

microwaving some leftovers for her dinner. It had been nearly a week since she left Boston and while she was able to fairly keep up with things at the office and keep them in the loop, she had an inbox overflowing with emails and voice messages. She'd take care of what she could and spend a couple hours tomorrow morning while her mother was getting her treatment dealing with the things that required real-time discussion. It was well after 10 before she finally went to bed, utterly spent.

On Sunday they decided to swing by the bakery before heading on their way to chemo that afternoon. After that first day, Patty was prescribed a different antiemetic and her body seemed to be adjusting to everything a bit better. She was still weak and tired and sick feeling, but it wasn't nearly as bad as it was at first. Never one to sit at home for long periods, they were both going a bit stir crazy between sitting in the hospital chairs and sitting at home. She needed to get out and do something else for a few minutes; plus, it was a great excuse to pick up some bread and other items to take home and check in on her business. There was very little argument from Elizabeth on this point because she knew how important the bakery was to Patty and she could relate to her mother's need to keep tabs. They would have to stick to the office and the kitchen area to avoid the germs in the dining area and nearer the counter from all the customers, but Patty didn't mind. She had her mask and giant squirt bottle of hand sanitizer at the ready.

They parked Patty's old Chevy truck in the parking area behind the building and entered through the back door, passing through a small hallway that held the pantry, a door into the walk-in and the door to Patty's small office before opening into the 2000 square foot main area filled with different workstations and appliances as well as several strategically placed ovens and ranges. The front of the kitchen area was separated from the display area and dining room by a large glass wall that had a counter running its length holding the coffee and cappuccino makers, cups, bowls, paper plates, soup warmers, the bread slicer and other items necessary to carry out the daily operation of serving customers. A few feet separated this cabinet from the service counter which was comprised of various display cases and refrigerated boxes that held the selection of pastries, cakes, pies, cookies, muffins, sandwich items and prepackaged lunches and drinks and so on.

Affixed to the partition were 3 large blackboards, reachable by standing on the counter-top, that contained the various menus and prices as well as specials and limited time items listed out in bright colors. Beyond the service area was the dining room comprised of a number of tables and chairs and a cream and sugar station where patrons could doctor their coffees and teas. Along one wall in this area was a rack of baskets containing the day's bread bagged up and ready for sale as well as discounted items from the previous day. In the warmer months, there are also tables and chairs with umbrellas out along the front of the building on the very wide brick sidewalk.

In the counter service and dining area, there were 6 employees bustling about to perform various duties: making sandwiches, wiping down tables, making coffee drinks, emptying trashes, rotating and filling stock, getting the side-work done, serving customers. There was a large tip jar on the counter in front of the register and it was nearly always full when it was busy. Taped to the front of the jar was a scrap of paper that in brightly colored hand written letters said, 'River Rock Scholarship Fund.'

They arrived during the lull between the early morning church crowd and the lunch rush. Things would slow down considerably around 2pm.

The kitchen was bustling as well, each station abuzz with the work of making cookies and breads and cakes and various other food items. Some were preparing doughs for the next day, others were applying icings and glazes and such, finishing custom orders and so on. As they entered the hallway, Patty and Elizabeth were inundated with the various smells of cooking and immediately Elizabeth was transported back to her childhood.

"I'm just going to go into my office real quick and look over the receipts and orders from the last week and see if I need to add my signature to anything. Why don't you pick out a few things to bring home with us and visit with people for a spell – and can you please send Jake in here, I'd like to catch up with him." Patty was obviously not feeling all that well, the pallor of her skin and the tired sag at the corner of her eyes mimicked by the slump of her shoulders told Elizabeth that this would be a short visit at least.

"Sure Mom – do you want anything special from the front?" She had serious doubts that coming here at all had been a good idea for Patty, but there was no way she'd deny her mother something so simple.

"You know what I like, Ellie. Nothing tastes right anymore, so I'm sure whatever you pick out will be ok." She offered her daughter a weak smile that looked more like a grimace and turned into her office.

Elizabeth continued through to the kitchen area

and was greeted by waves and warm smiles. She recognized a few of the senior staff from previous visits and she stopped by their stations to chat with them each briefly getting updates about their families and daily lives, giving them updates on Patty and herself, getting reintroduced to the rest of the staff, thanking people for their various offers of help through this time and so on. She made her way up to the front of the store finding Jake sitting in the dining area chatting up some customers. He looked up and excused himself from the table and made his way back behind the counter and greeted Elizabeth with a hug, his long frame and wide shoulders engulfing her in a comforting embrace.

Jake Wilson had been the general manager of the front end operations at River Rock for six years and in that time was able to fill extended hours in the summer, fall and holiday weeks by including live local music from Thursday through Saturday night, increasing the overall profit by 15%. Originally from Chama, New Mexico Jake moved to the area with his wife, Abby, who was originally from Glenwood Springs. They met at UNM Taos in the humanities department.

"Hey, Ellie- it's good to see you. Did you bring Patty with you? How is she?" He kept an arm around her and they walked together through the glass doors away from the customer's ears. He pulled up a couple stools and sat them near the warm ovens in an otherwise empty corner of the room.

"Hi Jake, it's good to see you too. She's in the office- she asked to see you. She's doing alright- as well as can be expected I guess." She shrugged and tried not to looked too worried. "This'll be day four of chemo and she seems to have evened out some by morning anyhow. It's been rough, but she's a trooper, you know?" He nodded his understanding and agreement.

"How are you holding up?" Jake had always been a caring sensitive guy, and Elizabeth knew he asked because he really wanted to know and not because it was the polite thing to do. So, she answered honestly.

"It's been rough...hard on both of us, but I'm not going to complain about it. If this is what we need to do to beat this thing, this is what we're going to do. That's all there is to it, really. I hate it that she's sick. I hate it that the 'cure' is making her feel worse- I hate seeing her like this, knowing there's nothing I can do beyond what I'm doing but that's just it. You can't do more than what you're able to do and if all 1 can be is strong then that's what I've gotta be. She sure as hell is. Whatever I'm feeling isn't nearly what she's going through and that knowledge helps me keep perspective- I hope. So far, anyway – but that's enough about me. How are you? How are Abby and that little boy of yours?"

At the mention of his wife and 7 month old son Bailey his face transformed from an expression of concern to one of beaming pride. "They are doing great. You wouldn't believe how big Bailey's getting! And he's crawling like a pro and he's trying to talk now but that's slow going for him – it mostly comes out as gibberish but he can say 'mama' and 'dada' now- sometimes," He chuckled. "As much as I can't wait to be able to throw the football with him and take him hiking and teach him all about the world around him, I'm kind of enjoying him as he is, you know? It's amazing, Elle. They come into this world so small and so fragile and so completely dependent on you...really just kind of a little person shaped blob with not a lot going on, you know? Crying, eating, puking, sleeping, shitting on a repeat cycle but eventually little changes take shape and all of a sudden there's a little personality emerging and you get glimpses of who he's gonna be. I can't even begin to describe it." In talking about his son his eyes were sparkling, his carriage was straighter, his chest was puffed out more; his love and pride in his family was obvious and for a split second Elizabeth felt a pang of jealousy. *Oh how wonderful it would have been to have a father even half as great as Jake.* But that was only part of it. It would be so nice to have someone to be happy with, to be proud of, to be loved by in return the way Jake had Abby. *Where did that come from?* She mentally shook herself back into the now.

"Well it sounds like fatherhood suits you well, Jake. I'm glad you and Abby were finally able to achieve this. That little boy is blessed to have you both."

Jake and Abby had been trying off and on to have a baby for a couple years and the last time they stopped trying it just happened. Elizabeth doubted two people have ever been happier than Jake and Abby when they announced the news. Luckily, she had been visiting her mother at the time and got to congratulate the couple in person.

"How is Abby? Has she gone back to work yet?"

"She's doing really well, actually- thanks for asking. She'll start back to work in August when the new school year begins. She really wanted to spend Bailey's first year with him as much as possible and I'm glad the college held her position, but to be honest, I think she's going a bit stir crazy." He smiled and rose from his stool, "Well, I'd better get back there and visit with your mom a bit- I'm sure she's wondering what we've been getting up to these past several days." He took a step toward the office and turned back, "Oh, before I forget- Abby wanted me to let you know that she's got Tuesdays and Saturdays free since her parents take Bailey for the day. If you ever need anything, she wanted you to know you can call her- 'even if you just need someone to come by and vacuum or whatever.' Same goes for me, but you already know that- or you should by now!" He reached out and squeezed her shoulder gently with one of his beefy hands and turned to walk away before she could thank him for the offer. She smiled to herself and just shook her head as she went back out to the front of the store.

"Elizabeth Thornton, is that you?" The rich deep voice sent a shiver down her spine and she turned her gaze to find a tall, vaguely familiar and ruggedly handsome blond man with piercing blue eyes smiling at her. He was at least 6'3", his broad shoulders tapering down into a trim waist. His red button down shirt was tucked neatly into a pair of worn Levi's. He appeared to be roughly her age, and she blinked at him a few times digging through her memory trying to place the chiseled face with the people she grew up with.

He laughed, "You don't remember me, do you?" She shook her head. "Charlie Moore- Shelly's little brother? I was a couple years behind you but you used to come over to our house from time to time and study or hang out with Shelly."

A wide smile of recognition emerged on her face and she went around the counter to greet him properly. "Oh my God, Charlie Moore...just look at you all grown up!" They pulled each other into a quick hug and then stepped apart but within arms length.

"What are you doing in town? I thought you were one of the few who got out?" He approached the counter with his beverage, glanced at the girl waiting there and pointed to something in the case indicating two and returned his gaze to Elizabeth.

He must not spend much time in town if he hasn't already heard. The last thing I want right now is more sympathy. "I'm just visiting with Mom for a few weeks. How about you - what's happening in your life these days? How are Shelly and the rest of the Moore clan?"

Charlie put the change from his purchase into the tip jar and gave his server a wink before asking Elizabeth to sit with him a few minutes and catch up some. It didn't escape Elizabeth's notice how the girl practically danced through the glass doors into the kitchen area. She looked at Charlie with one eyebrow raised and he laughed.

They exchanged a few bits of information about each other and she learned all about Shelly leaving her husband taking her 2 kids with her about a year ago and moving back home and about how their dad fell off the barn roof a couple weeks back and broke his leg and so on. Finally, Charlie looked at his watch and said, "Oh my, Elle it's been great talking with you but I've gotta go, I'm very late for a meeting." He smiled apologetically and pushed back from the table, stood up, and placed his hand warmly over hers. He looked her in the eye and said, "I really hope we can do this again sometime."

"I'd like that, Charlie." She smiled up at him. "Thanks for the chat- and tell Shelly and your folks I said hi."

"Will do…take care Elle," and with that he was gone.

Later that night, laying in bed Elizabeth allowed her mind to roam freely over the events of the past few days. As she drifted off to sleep, two faces were swirling around in her minds eye.

Chapter 20

Tuesday night, Hailey awoke panting, her body trapped and twisted by sweat soaked sheets, hair plastered to her face and neck. A strange confusion of images fading as awareness seeped in. At first she didn't know where she was and it took several seconds for her to realize that she was in her own bed. It was always the same dream or at least the same theme when she woke up like this. It didn't happen very often, really only in times of stress. Hailey would be feeling intense love and warmth and pleasure only to have it shrink away from her. She would search for it, chase it, but in the end there was nothing but a choking emptiness. It was the same feeling that squeezed her heart when her father died; when her Nonna died; when her mother left; whenever she thought about Fitch or even Gen in the beginning. It didn't take a therapist to tell her that this dream was tied into her abandonment issues.

The clock on her bedside table read 3:19 am.

"Looks like it's time to get up. It's not like I need sleep anyway. Maybe I can get some work done, at least." She rose up out of the bed and walked into the bathroom where she took a quick cool shower, got dressed and started for her studio.

Chapter 21

"Mom, are you alright? Can I get you anything?" Elizabeth was leaning with her head against the bathroom door and Patty was inside vomiting again, it was just past 3pm on Tuesday- the last day of the first round of chemo and in a couple days they would go in for a few tests to see how well it was all working.

"Maybe just a glass of water, please, Ellie." Her voice was small and weak sounding and Elizabeth had to strain to hear it. She opened the door at the same time Patty flushed the toilet yet again, the smell in the room sour, but not as bad as it could have been. Over the past several days they had learned that the more bland the food the easier the whole process- if Patty would eat at all. She had lost at least 10 pounds if not more from her already thin frame, all of her clothes were beginning to hang loosely on her body and she joked that she'd be able to wear the clothes she had saved from her younger days again pretty soon. Elizabeth had laughed along, but she certainly didn't think it was funny.

She handed Patty a moistened paper towel to wipe her face with then held a plastic tumbler filled with water and a straw up to her lips for her to drink. When it appeared that Patty would be keeping the water down for a bit, she helped her to her feet and walked her back to her room where Patty returned to her bed. Elizabeth then went and got a cold wet rag and placed it on Patty's hot forehead.

"Hopefully in a couple days we'll see some results from all this, Mom. You're doing great, just hang in there." Patty was already asleep.

Elizabeth padded out into the sunroom, held a pillow from the sofa up to her face and cried for a long time. *Please don't let this be all for nothing.*

Chapter 22

The following Friday afternoon, Hailey showed up at Patty's as was her new habit. She hadn't missed many days stopping by since the diagnosis and had even spent a couple mornings sitting with her through her chemo while Elizabeth ran errands, did chores and did work related stuff.

As hard as it was for Hailey to be reminded of Nonna and seeing Patty going through the same things, she wouldn't miss the opportunity to spend time with her good friend- especially since that time seemed so limited.

"Knock, knock?" Hailey poked her head in through the front door and called into the house.

"We're in here- come on back, Hailey."

Hailey entered into the living room carrying her ever present backpack. Her hair was pulled back into a pony tail and her cheeks were pink from the chill. She was wearing sturdy shoes, jeans and a light wind-resistant shell over a couple other light layers. On her head she wore a lightweight knit cap.

"Goodness, look at you! Did you walk here?" Patty came around and gave Hailey a hug. "Oh my, your cheeks are cold!"

Hailey looked at Elizabeth, smiled and shrugged as Patty led her further into the room. "Yes, I walked! It's gorgeous outside! In fact, I was hoping to steal Elizabeth away for a couple hours – I thought I might show her my shop if you really are feeling better and not just pulling my leg."

"Oh that sounds like a fun idea- Ellie?" Both Hailey and Patty looked at Elizabeth expectantly, Hailey with a slight grin and sparkling eyes, Patty with eyebrows raised in question.

"Oh, I don't know…It's really up to Mom. *Are you feeling better this morning?*" She searched her mother's face for any sign that she should stay and saw none. Certainly Patty tired more easily, sure she wasn't as strong and didn't feel like eating much but she was definitely in high spirits today and her color was starting to return to her cheeks even if only slightly, so Elizabeth allowed herself to feel the hope her mother was broadcasting.

"Oh don't be silly- I can take care of myself for a few hours- besides it'll allow me to catch up on my reading. You go on, I'll be fine."

"Before I forget," Hailey said as she reached into her bag, pulling out a small black drawstring bag and handing it to Patty. "Here are those clippers you wanted to borrow." She glanced apologetically to Elizabeth and offered a small smile to Patty.

"Thanks, Dear. I'm glad you had these. I don't think we've ever had a pair of hair clippers in the house, have we Ellie?" She tucked the bag under her arm. "I'm going to get myself something to chew on – would either of you like anything while I'm at it?"

Hailey held up her full water bottle in response and Elizabeth also declined turning to Hailey with a quizzical expression on her face, "Clippers?"

"She called me yesterday asking if I had a pair of hair clippers. Said she noticed an unusually large amount of hair in the drain after her shower and I think she wants to take control of that part of it before it starts to really come out on its own. Don't worry, Elizabeth. This is a very common part of it and it's very personal for her. It's amazing how much of a woman's identity is tied up in her hair. So this will probably be very hard for her. If she doesn't want to share the actual cutting, don't be offended. The best you can do is tell her how beautiful she is after the fact."

Elizabeth regarded Hailey closely for a few moments; hurt, anger, sadness and resignation all crossing her own features as she processed everything Hailey just told her. "You seem to know an awful lot about all this." It was more a question than a statement and she regarded Hailey for a few more moments. Hailey's expression darkened for a moment and she looked away. "You've been through it?" She guessed.

Hailey returned her gaze for a moment, the sadness still churning at the corners of her eyes and nodded. "With my Nonna."

Before either could say anything further Patty returned to the room carrying a drink and a bowl of dry Chex cereal. "I just remembered, Ellie. Riley has a vet appointment tomorrow morning to get his shots all updated- do you mind taking him?"

"No I don't mind, Mom. You can just tell me where I need to go and I'll do it. It might be a good opportunity to get some grocery shopping done too, so if you need anything let me know- maybe you can make a list if reading doesn't suit your fancy while we're checking out Hailey's shop?"

"That sounds like a great idea- I definitely need some more lotion, my skin has been so dry! And we're nearly out of Gatorade. I was thinking that we should get some of the powder and just mix our own- it'll probably last longer that way." Elizabeth just nodded.

They sat around talking for a while longer, until Patty started to nod off. Elizabeth reached out and gently squeezed her foot. "Hey Mom, Hailey and I are going to go now – do you need anything before we head out?"

"No, you go ahead and run along dear – I think I'll just stay here and take a little nap." She smiled affectionately at her daughter as Elizabeth placed a blanket over her lower half.

"Ok Mom – I'll just go let Riley back in and we'll be off then. I'll be back for dinner and I'll have my cell phone if you need me to come home."

"I can let Riley in if you want to put on some heavier shoes and a jacket?" Hailey offered.

"Is it cold out?"

"Well it's definitely chilly and there's some mud in places. It'll be a bit colder on the way back; with the sun just on the other side of the ridge the temperature usually drops a good amount. In fact I'll probably just drive you, but it'll still be chilly on the way there- it's a couple miles."

"Ok. You're probably right- I'll meet you up front."

~~~

"Thanks for suggesting this, Hailey. I needed to get my blood pumping; it's been too long." Elizabeth and Hailey were walking side by side along the road between their respective homes. To their right the land rose up to form a ridge dotted with various scrub brush and trees which the edge of sun was beginning to tease, casting a widening shadow along the side of the road.

On the opposite side was the winding Crystal River swollen from the melting snow. The air was crisp and calm and the sky was pale blue with hardly a trace of clouds. Some early wildflowers had already blossomed, the grass had begun to come alive and the leaves on few deciduous trees and bushes were beginning to unfurl from their buds; the colors painting the valley were breathtaking.

"Yea, I like to get out and walk or hike at least once a week- I wish I had time to do it more. I usually ride a bike or swim for exercise but that's not a really great way to just relax and enjoy the countryside the way a nice long hike or even a drive can be. It's nice to just take it all in, sometimes, you know- especially since I get most of my inspiration from nature."

"I know what you mean. I run 5 miles a day and do Pilates but it's not the same. Lately when I'm walking in Boston it's to get from one place to another in the city. I used to take weekend trips into the mountains just to feel closer to home, but I haven't had time to do that in quite a while." Her tone had become wistful recalling the general turn of her life back in Boston. While she wasn't unhappy, if she actually gave it any thought she wouldn't say that she was content. There were several areas in her life that she would prefer to have differently, but she didn't know what more she could do to have it without risking everything she'd worked so hard for. Her work was her life and as long as that remained rewarding she'd have to be satisfied and everything else would get put on the shelf labeled 'someday.'

"So I noticed you didn't refer to Boston as 'home.'" Hailey ventured.

Is it me or does she sound hopeful? "Well this is where I grew up, it's where my family is- as long as that's true this will be home." Elizabeth went silent as it dawned on her that this might not always be true. *Oh my God.*

Picking up on this fact, Hailey decided that perhaps some silence was needed and just let the quiet sink in around them for a few minutes. She reached out a tentative hand and gave Elizabeth's shoulder a squeeze when a small motion caught her eye.

"Oh my goodness! Look at that!" Hailey was pointing at something off to the side of the road. "Wow – I almost didn't see it."

"What? Where? Oh! A box turtle! What's he doing here on the side of the road? This isn't really a good place for you to live, little guy."

They moved off the road more and bent to get a better look at the animal, noting his high domed shell and his yellow and green markings.

"It's not too far to my house now and there's plenty of space out back that he might like...Do you think we should move him?"

"Well, I would hate for him to get run over. I don't think it would hurt him to pick him up, do you?"

Their eyes met and they smiled at each other. Elizabeth bent to pick the tortoise up and they put their heads together to get a closer look as the animal pulled in its tail head and limbs and the shell closed tight.

Hailey gently ran a finger along its 'belly', "What shall we call you?"

They resume walking. "How about Terry? It is a terrapene, after all and Terry's pretty gender neutral."

"Terry the turtle…that has a nice ring to it. I love

it!" Her smile was wide and bright and reached all the way up to her sparkling blue eyes. Not for the first time did Elizabeth notice how beautiful her new friend was. She flashed a brilliant smile of her own to match.

"I know just the place to release him. That's my drive just ahead."

They turned off the main road onto a single unpaved lane that wound its way for about 30 yards up to a two story Frank Lloyd Wright inspired house made of wood and stone, partially cut into the hill on one side and surrounded by transplanted trees and a freshly sodden lawn.

As they approached the home, Elizabeth noted the impressive number of large windows.

"Let's take Terry around the house – I'll meet you back there, I'm just gonna grab something from my shop." Hailey jogged ahead and entered a rather large structure made of similar materials as the house, with nearly as many windows. On the side of the building there were 2 large garage style doors, large enough to fit 2 cars side by side and it looked like the wall on the end opened up as well *That must be how she gets her pieces out of there...*

Elizabeth stepped into the backyard and was brought up short, her breath caught in her throat. At least a dozen different fruit trees all in various stages of budding were scattered over the large yard, as well as various shrubs and flowering plants strategically placed along walkways and other features. Another building of stone and wood encased almost entirely in glass sat off on the far end, attached to the house via a large patio and pergola that housed an outdoor kitchen and sitting area as well as what looked like a hot tub area. As in the front, so too the back of the house where there wasn't a patio or walkway were large flowerbeds abutting the house, all freshly mulched and very much alive with a variety of different types of bulbs and ground cover and other flowering plants hinting at the cascade of textures and colors that would mark the summer months. The ground had a fairly pronounced slope to it and this was used to create a series of waterfalls that terminated into a roughly 10' x 15' koi pond in the center of the yard, filled with various water plants and several multicolored fish.

"You like it?" Hailey asked softly. Elizabeth startled by the closeness and the warm breath near her ear and turned to find herself being appraised by Hailey, an amused expression on her face.

"Are you kidding? It's beautiful." *Was she just checking me out?* This almost came out as a whisper such was the awe that she was feeling just looking at this space.

"Well, thank you," she said a bit shyly, suddenly a bit self conscious by Elizabeth's reaction. "When I sat down with the architect, I wanted to utilize the natural beauty of the area and create an oasis for myself where I can enjoy living and working and find constant inspiration. I think we did alright."

Elizabeth could only nod agreement, and feeling a bit awkward she held out the turtle. "Alright then, where do you want Terry to live?"

Hailey chuckled and gently took the tortoise from her explaining, "Well, I thought maybe we should just put her down anywhere back here and let her decide. But first I wanted to put a small mark on her shell so we could tell it's her if she decides to stick around or come back." With this she produced the paint marker that she fetched from her shop and instructed Elizabeth to put a mark on the shell where it wouldn't wear off easily. Once this was done, they gently placed Terry in the grass and walked away.

"Would you like something to drink?"

"That would be nice. Actually, I need to use the restroom- do you mind?"

She laughed, "Of course not – here I'll show you where it is and when you're finished I'll give you the nickel tour." She smiled and led Elizabeth into her home.

In the bathroom Elizabeth examined herself in the mirror, chiding herself for the thoughts she was having about Hailey. It wouldn't be the first woman she'd been attracted to, and certainly not the first she'd been with if things lead down that path but there was something about Hailey that stirred something long dormant within her, something that she didn't recognize. There was a depth to her, a sadness that touched Elizabeth like no one else has.

This can't happen now…what about Mom? You can't just go off and have a fling like this when Mom's so sick. And she's Mom's friend for Chrissakes! And one of the few people you may call a real friend too… What if things didn't work out? And you don't even know if Hailey's even remotely interested, anyway. But oh my God, she's gorgeous! And sexy… I wonder what it would feel like to rub our bodies- stop it, Elizabeth, stop it right now! This cannot happen! You'll just have to find someone that's not so close if you need a release. "Damn it, anyway."

~~~

"You have a beautiful home, Hailey. I don't

think I've ever seen one quite like it." Hailey was a gracious host, offering explanations for the various elements and materials used in her home, answering Elizabeth's questions, even preparing a snack of cottage cheese and fresh fruit to go with the peach iced tea they were drinking. Her home was an elegant mix of metal, wood, stone and glass, decorated sparingly with rich colors and textures that complimented the space in a way that the overall effect made the home feel like a warm embrace.

"Thanks. I like it." She laughed and started walking toward the kitchen and out to the shop area. "Not a lot of people have been out here - it's kind of my best kept secret." 'Or one of them, anyway,' she mutters to her self.

"What was that?"

"Huh? Oh- I was just wondering if Terry's still out here." Hailey made a beeline for where they dropped Terry the Turtle off in her yard to find it just a few feet away, nearer the water.

"I don't blame him for wanting to stay."

"Yea, we'll see...Hey – you ready to see what I'm working on?"

"Absolutely – lead the way! This is the sculpture you're creating for that park in your hometown, right?"

"Yep – that's one of them. Come on, I'll show you." The sparkle of excitement and mischief was dancing in her eyes as she grabbed Elizabeth's hand and led her into her expansive workspace.

The shop itself was incredible; well over 2500 square feet of floor space, with 20'high ceilings it looked more like a half gymnasium than a barn or shop.

Other than the doors, the walls appeared to be solid 12 foot high expanses of stone and wood, the remaining 8 feet to the ceiling encased in glass to allow the natural light in. The ceiling was an echo of the flat roof seen from outside and contained several skylights and large wooden beams as well as suspended lighting and a couple sturdy looking chain and pulley hoist set ups.

Along every single available wall space within were various work benches, shelves, racks and cabinets containing a wide variety of tools, machines, materials and other necessary implements of Hailey's trade. Spread out along the center of the room were 3 distinct lumps of varying size each covered by a heavy canvas tarp.

"Wow, Hailey- this is quite a workshop."

"Yea, it's pretty awesome. I especially love all the windows and skylights...they let in so much light and being able to see the sky really lets me feel less trapped inside."

"Are these your current pieces?" Elizabeth let go of Hailey's hand and stepped away, immediately feeling the loss of warmth and pointed to the 3 large tarp covered lumps knowing that they are most likely works in various state of progress.

"Yes – here let me show you." Hailey smiled brightly and walked over to the first lump and pulled at the tarp, causing it to cascade onto the floor where she bunched it into a pile and kicked it aside. As she was doing this, she was acutely aware of Elizabeth's presence, of her gasping reaction to the piece, of her circling scrutiny of her work.

"Oh my God, Hailey – this is beautiful." Her voice was nearly a whisper as she slowly circled the piece. She glanced over at Hailey who was standing awkwardly to the side obviously self conscious, a blush was teasing at her shirt collar threatening to overtake her. The piece depicted a mare and her foal in a snapshot of playful glee and it was made out of what appeared to be various bits and pieces of scrap metal shaped and welded together. The meticulous attention to detail was such that if not for the spots of paint and rust and the odd spring or nut or bolt or tire rim that remained exposed it wouldn't be obvious that recycled materials were used until observed from close range.

"It's not finished yet but I prefer it in this state." She reached out her hand and fondly touched the face of the foal. "Of course, the client has a different idea about it but I like the fact that you can see what some of the scraps I used used to be. I think the splashes of color and rust give it added character." She sighed and dropped her hand back to her side and continued to pace around her work eyeing it critically. "From here it'll get sent to the sand-blaster's where all the rust and paint and any spurs will be removed and then it'll get a powder-coating in matte black to cover the welds and protect the piece from the elements."

"I like it the way it is now too; for something stationary you certainly were able to capture a wonderful sense of motion. Where will it live when it's complete?"

Hailey looked at Elizabeth and smiled. She murmured, "I like how you worded that…like it's alive…that's nice." She took a deep breath and looked back at the piece, "They're going to 'live' on a luxury dude ranch and spa in Montana." She walked over to the next tarpaulin covered piece and asked, "Can you give me a hand with this?"

Together they pulled the tarp off the second sculpture, this time it was the patinaed copper sheet metal model for the abstract sea piece they discussed a few days ago.

"It's only a quarter of the size that the finished bronze will be, but I think you can get a sense of what I'm aiming for with this one." The curves and curls of the metal reached up and out to gradually become ripples that disappeared into a smooth base and from every angle it looked like rolling and crashing waves almost as if in a passing storm.

"Wow, Hailey this is really amazing; you've managed to invoke a feeling of both power and serenity at the same time." She reached out to touch it, running her fingertips and then her palm along one of the curves in a long caress. "It's a similar feeling I get when I'm looking at the ocean- the vastness and awesome destructive and life giving power that makes me feel small in the larger universe and the soothing sound of the waves that provides a calm sense of peacefulness. I can only imagine it at full size and fully weathered." Elizabeth looked from the sculpture to Hailey, whose eyes had been tracking Elizabeth's hand on the work with an expression bordering hunger that Elizabeth almost didn't catch. She stepped a bit closer to Hailey and said softly, "You're very talented."

Hailey cleared her throat and brought her gaze up to Elizabeth's eyes and then quickly glanced to the large clock on the wall, her eyes widening in surprise. *If I didn't know any better, Hailey I'd say I make you nervous.*

"Oh my goodness, is it really almost 6 o'clock- Patty must be starting to worry. I should take you home." She didn't make eye contact again with

Elizabeth and instead abruptly started walking to the door, waiting there only long enough for Elizabeth to exit the building before turning out the lights and practically jogging to her jeep. *Where's the fire, Hailey?*

~~~

They rode in near silence and when they got to Elizabeth's only the porch light was on. Hailey figured Patty retired for the evening and went back home, thanking Elizabeth for the afternoon before she sped back down the road.

Once in the house, Elizabeth let Riley out and found a note on the fridge from Patty letting her know that she'd already eaten some leftovers and was now in bed. She grabbed a yogurt and a spoon and sat at the bar until it was time to bring Riley back in. In the hallway she saw some light coming through the bottom of Patty's door and knocked gently.

"Come in."

"Hi Mom. I just wanted to see how you're-" She stopped short. Patty had shaved her head and where once a glorious wild mane of gorgeous copper and auburn hair was, nothing but a pale bald scalp, which made her features stand out all the more starkly, her eyes red from crying looked even larger. She walked further into the room. "Wow! Going punk rock, I see." She fought hard to hide the shock and inject some levity, certain that her mother was hurting and self conscious over losing her hair.

"Ha ha!" She sniffed. "Is that what you call this?" She pointed to her head.

"Hell yes! It's bad ass." She sat on the edge of the bed and gently rubbed her mother's scalp. "You've got the head for it too- nice and round, no strange lumps to throw it off balance. Just think of all the money we'll save on shampoo now." She looked into her mother's face, her eyes, tried to telepathically broadcast every ounce of love she could. "You're beautiful, Mom and I love you. Not because as your daughter I have to, but because you're an amazing and wonderful person."

Tears were streaking silently down Patty's face. "You're the best daughter and friend a person could ever hope for."

"It's only hair, it's not who you are."

She was crying now, and Elizabeth crawled onto the bed next to her and held her until her sobs subsided, until her breathing became steady, until she drifted off to sleep.

Chapter 23

"Ms. Thornton, you can go ahead and take Riley into exam room number 3- right through there and it's the second door on the left. The doctor will be in shortly." The receptionist/ vet tech indicated a large double door and gave Elizabeth and Riley a warm smile that crinkled the corners of her eyes. The office itself is obviously new, everything still had that just installed shine and the place still smelled vaguely of paint.

The door to the exam room was standing ajar and Elizabeth lead Riley in. In the center of the room seemingly coming out of the wall stood a large steel topped exam table that housed a series of drawers and cabinet doors below. On one wall there was a digital scale made for animals and along the walls there were posters and info-graphics enumerating the various things to pay attention to pertaining to the health of your pet. On a third wall there were cabinets and a small sink area and on the countertops there were various containers of treats and swabs and purple nitrile gloves and such.

The vet entered the exam room while leafing through Riley's chart, "Looks like we're just doing a routine annual exam and some shots, is that right, Riley? Oh! It's you!" Charlie Moore looked up from Riley's chart and saw Elizabeth eyeing him with an amused expression.

"It's me. And you're a *Doctor* now, huh?"

He blushed and came further into the room. "Yea – well not a doctor doctor...like a people doctor..." He rushed on and finally screwed up his confidence. "I mean…yea, I am a doctor, and probably better off than if I'd stuck to regular med school."

"Oh?"

"Well, yea – most of the people in my pre-med classes were only there because their fathers were doctors or because they wanted the money and the prestige. Very few were actually interested in helping people and I'd had enough of them the first 4 years that I knew I didn't want to spend the next 4 years with them too. A few of my pre-med classes had a lot to do with animals, and considering I grew up on a farm it seemed the best logical alternative and now I get to save lives on a regular basis and my patients and their people are generally happy." He shrugged.

"Well I think it's great, Charlie. I'm sure Riley appreciates it too." She bent over and scratched the dog behind the ears affectionately. "How long have you been in practice?"

As they spoke, he conducted his exam of Riley, pausing here and there to write notes into Riley's file and so on. "Well, technically I've been practicing veterinary medicine for a little over 8 months. This is my first practice- and hopefully my last. Although I did spend every summer and weekend interning at a place near my Alma Mater, which in addition to my scholarships and other financial aid is how I was able to graduate without debt and start this place. I've been pretty lucky that way I guess." He smiled.

"That's really cool Charlie- way to go. Your parents must be glad to have you back in the area."

"Yea, they are and with Shelly and the kids and everything that's been going on with them and now with Dad, I'm glad I can be here to help out too. It takes some of the strain off Mom, you know? You should stop by there one of these days. I bet they'd love to catch up with you."

She nodded at his suggestion. "I just might do that. So what about a Mrs. Charlie Moore?" she asked with an arched eyebrow.

"Ha! No, there's no one like that just now. I mean, there've been a few that might have been but weren't, you know? And I'm not desperate for company if you know what I mean," He winked. "I guess between being completely absorbed with getting an education and launching my practice and trying to learn from Shelly's mistake I just haven't given myself the time to settle down- besides, I'm kind of enjoying being unfettered in that department. What about you? I don't see a ring on your finger," He teased.

"Oh, it's like you said. Busy with school, busy taking over the world. Not enough time or interest to get serious with anyone, really. There've been flings over the years but never even a maybe, really. My life is neat and that's how I like it."

His eyes met hers and he looked at her for a few moments, "Can I take you out to dinner sometime while you're here? Or lunch? Or breakfast?" With this he wagged his eyebrows playfully.

"You just cut right to the chase, don't you Charlie," She teased. If she's being honest with herself, she had definitely given some thought to having a no strings interlude with the ruggedly handsome Charlie Moore. *Would it be weird to get it on with someone you practically grew up with? I mean, I knew him as a kid...is that strange? Nah.*

He studied her face as the different thoughts

flitted across it, "Hey it doesn't have to be a date if you're uncomfortable, I was just kidding." "I'd love to, Charlie." They spoke at the same time and laughed when they realized what the other said.

"You would?"

"Yes. I would love to have dinner and maybe breakfast with you." She spoke softly and gave him full eye contact and a playful smile.

"Wow, you just cut right to the chase, don't you Elle." He smiled at her, light dancing in his eyes. *He really is a sexy man.*

"As long as you understand that I'm not looking for anything serious and I'll probably only be in the area for a short while, it could be fun. But, I want to be clear; I don't want you to think this could lead to something more than that. And I don't want things to get weird between us- if you can't handle that, then I'd have to decline."

"Don't worry, Elle. I'm a big boy now, and I think we're on the same page." He reached out and placed his hand on her hand and they stood like that for a few moments just looking at each other.

"Alright then." And then a thought occurred to her, "You don't still live with your parents do you?"

"Ha Ha! No, I've got my own place – God can you imagine?" His laugh was hearty and deep and he shook his head. "No, I'd never get anywhere with anyone if I lived with them. Besides, I've been on my own for too long to go back now."

"Ah, that's good. Hotels can be so awkward." She deadpanned and laughed as his jaw dropped.

~~~

"Hey Mom! We're back!"

"I'm back here, Ellie."

Elizabeth released Riley from his leash and he ran off ahead of her toward Patty and the back of the house. She stopped in the kitchen to grab herself some water, "Do you need anything from the kitchen?"

"No I'm good, thanks." She called back.

Full water glass in hand she made her way through the house and to the back where the bedrooms and extra rooms were hidden. "Where are you?"

"I'm in here, Sweetie," She called. "Riley you stinker get down already you scamp!" she said with a laugh.

She followed the voice down the hallway to the last room on the right, where she stepped through the open doorway to find her mother flushed and out of breath, pulling a drop cloth off a pile in the far corner of the room.

"Hey Mom, let me help you with that – what are you doing back here anyway? You should be resting."

"I get tired of sitting or laying around all day, Ellie. Besides, I got to thinking about things and wanted to dig some of this stuff out."

"Is that what I think it is?"

"Yep – it's all your old paintings and supplies. Remember how much you used to love to paint? I never did understand why you stopped...you were always so talented." She rifled through the stack of finished canvases and pulled one from the pile. "Ah – here it is. I think I'd like to hang this one over the fireplace. What do you think?" She asked holding out a landscape of Mount Sopris with the sunset reflected off the snow capped summit and the stars emerging in the darkening sky above. "I've always loved this one."

"Me too, but I also like the one you have hanging there now. Are you planning on keeping it up?"

"Well, actually I was thinking about giving it to Hailey for her birthday. Every time she comes over she spends at least 5 minutes just staring at it, so I know she'd like it – that is, if you don't mind. You left so many paintings here that I just assumed you didn't want them anymore." She continued to look through the stack, "You should sign these, Elizabeth. You never know what might happen someday."

For some reason it gave Elizabeth a warm feeling that someone as talented as Hailey might appreciate her art. She loved painting, and had been quite good back in her college days. Of course, anything creative that required her to expose something of her deeper self for the world to see made her uncomfortable so she didn't pursue gallery spots. She didn't enjoy being vulnerable, which is also why she never signed her work.

"When's her birthday?"

"It's in a couple weeks. I thought maybe we could get this cleaned up and that one wrapped by then...By the way, she's coming for dinner tonight instead of tomorrow. Apparently she has to go up to Oregon tomorrow and deal with the forge on that piece she's been working on and won't be back until Monday morning sometime."

"Ok – cool...I'll just go get cleaned up. I was also thinking that I should be adjusted to the altitude by now, so I'd like to start running again in the morning."

"That sounds like a good plan to me, Ellie. I'm going to leave these things a bit more accessible- maybe you'll get inspired to make me something new, hint hint." She smiled broadly at her daughter and pressed her hands together in the sign for 'please oh please with a cherry on top!' *It has been a long time…it might be fun…* "Maybe…"

Chapter 24

The music was pumping out a rhythm and bodies were writhing up against each other in the large cleared out living room of Zoë DioCosta's sprawling house. Once or twice a month she invited 20 or 30 of her closest friends over for a party that consisted of a pot luck followed by club night. Everyone chipped in 10$ for the DJ and they partied down until exhaustion claimed the last woman standing. Luckily a good portion of the female cops in the area that were off duty were in attendance, which helped keep the place from getting shut down because of the noise. Not that there were all that many neighbors to complain since Zoë's house sat in the center of nearly 100 acres.

"Hey beautiful. Haven't seen you in a while, How've you been?" Marci Hatcher never passed up an opportunity to hit on Hailey if she caught her alone. Hailey thought she was cute enough; she was five-foot-four, with a blonde pixie cut, crystal blue eyes, luscious kissable lips, pert breasts that would fit nicely in her palms and a body that knew the inside of a gym.

Hailey looked around for Zoë finally spotting her in a dark corner, her hands were travelling under the shirt of her toe-headed horse farmer, their lips locked in what looked to be an epic tongue battle.

"Do you want to dance?" Hailey offered her hand to Marci and when she took it they slipped into the crowd and began to move to the music. As their bodies inched closer and closer together Marci looked up into Hailey's eyes. Her gaze was met with a small grin and Hailey bent down to brush their lips together. There was no spark in that small effort so she pressed a little harder inviting more from Marci, thinking maybe it would just take a second. When she closed her eyes Elizabeth's face flashed before her eyes and she gasped. Marci was encouraged by this and slipped her tongue into the kiss, tracing Hailey's teeth and pulling Hailey's hips more firmly into her belly.

Hailey was the first to break contact, pulling away to look Marci in the eye. "I'm sorry Marci- you're a really beautiful woman, but I'm just not there. Forgive me?"

Marci pulled her into a hug, "She'd better not break your heart, whoever she is."

Hailey squeezed her shoulders once more and headed home.

Chapter 25

"Ok Patty, this is just going to pinch a bit and there will be a small prick." The obviously gay phlebotomist was mid to late 20's, wearing eggplant colored scrubs, had tattoo sleeves running both arms from wrist to somewhere past the cuff of her shirt. She had a lip piercing near the corner of her mouth and short spiky platinum blonde hair. Her eyes were the color of Honey and her name tag said 'Bobbi.' Elizabeth had seen plenty of her type marching up and down streets in Boston over the years, so the only surprise for her was how much the area had changed that this person could be proud and still get a professional job. Certainly Colorado was still a conservative part of the country, especially the rural areas and small towns. This seemed even more so when compared to Boston and New England for that matter, which was largely democratic and the origin of the 'Boston marriage' as well as several of the nation's first equal marriage rights laws.

Patty raised an eyebrow at the top of Bobbi's head as she bent over Patty's chest to draw the blood and glanced to Elizabeth who was watching the scene with an expression of amusement. *I wonder where else that skin's been inked...*

Bobbi was easily able to foster calm in Patty, making frequent eye contact. She smiled often and even flirted with them some, which made Patty giggle.

"Ok, that's the last tube Patty. I'm just going to tape this gauze down and then I'll take these down to the lab and start the tests. Dr. Martin should be with you shortly." As she left the room, she raised her eyes to Elizabeth's and smiled then quietly closed the door.

Patty arched an eyebrow at her daughter, "She seemed like a nice girl."

"Yea, she seemed to know what she was doing," She said vaguely, but the private double entendre amused her and she laughed inwardly. Patty looked like she wanted to say something else, but changed her mind. She shifted awkwardly on the exam table.

A light tapping on the door preceded the arrival of Dr. Martin. He stepped inside, gently closed the door and addressed the two women in the room. "Good Morning, Patty. Elizabeth." He crossed the room, chart in hand and sat in the blue rolling chair. Looking between the chart and Patty he continued. "Well you've been through one round of chemo. How was it?"

Patty snorted, "It was awful!" There was humor in her tone, but her answer was serious.

He nodded his understanding, "Yes according to our notes here you experienced various degrees of vomiting and nausea, diarrhea, joint stiffness, weakness, fatigue, fevers, chills…that's all par for the course with chemo. How do you feel now that it's been a couple weeks since your last treatment?"

"Well, I do still feel weak, and I tire easily. And my body still feels like it was run over by a truck, but I can keep simple foods down most of the time. And my skin is still so dry…I can't seem to get enough lotion." She said and shifted on her seat, pulling the edges of her gown more tightly closed as if the thin fabric could protect her from the situation.

Dr. Martin was nodding his head and writing down what she was telling him. He then set the folder and pen down on the counter and reached for the blood pressure cuff.

"Ok, well it doesn't seem like you're experiencing anything out of the ordinary and it's a good sign that your symptoms seem to have tapered some." He paused in his talking to count her pulse rate. "The dry skin is a common side effect, and my only recommendation is to hydrate from the inside as well as the outside. Besides the meds, you've been losing a lot of your water by being sick, so you actually need to drink more than normal." He removed the cuff from her arm and wrote the results into her file. "Blood pressure seems to be fine." He then reached for the otoscope. "Ok, we're just going to look into your ears...Ok, all good. Now your eyes... Follow my finger...Alright, now for your throat." He reached into a jar and grabbed a tongue depressor. "Alright then, open up and say 'AH.'"

"AH..."

"Hmmm..."

"Hmmm?"

"Have your gums been bleeding when you brush?"

"Yes, a little bit. Is that a problem?"

"Well, it might not be serious but it looks like your gums are irritated. Some patients experience periodontitis with some of the meds you're on and if left untreated it could lead to tooth loss and other more serious complications. This looks to be very early, but I don't want to take any chances. You will need to set up an appointment with your dentist for a cleaning and let them know what's going on. They will be able to provide treatment and recommend a good rinse and regiment to help keep this to a minimum."

She let out a long breath to steady herself. "Ok, we can call his office when we're done here." She looked to Elizabeth who nodded her head in agreement and offered a smile of encouragement.

"Alright now, Patty, I need to listen to your lungs…" Dr Martin continued to examine Patty, listening to the upper and lower lobes of her lungs and to her heartbeat from the front and the back. He palpated her abdomen and lymph nodes, checked her reflexes, talked about a couple bruises that he noticed on her thigh.

"Alright, Patty, I'll let you get dressed and then if you and Elizabeth would like to join me in my office where we can go over your lab and scan results; they should be finished by now." He squeezed Patty's shoulder on his way out.

"I'll just give you some privacy, Mom. Take your time." Elizabeth reached out and grabbed Patty's hand giving it a squeeze. Patty looked up at her with wide eyes. "I love you, Mom. I'm not going anywhere; we'll figure this out. I'll just be right outside this door."

"Ok, Ellie. I'll be right there." She gave a small smile that broke Elizabeth's heart.

The short corridor that connected the main office and reception areas with the exam rooms and doctors offices in the back was bustling with activity. Patients entering and exiting exam rooms, nurses and techs going about their daily duties all brought a certain life to the otherwise sterile place. Elizabeth looked over her shoulder and noticed Bobbi approaching with a small stack of folders in tow. Bobbi looked up and smiled at her.

"Hey. How is she?"

"You probably know better than we do just now."

At this she just shrugged and kept her features pleasant and optimistic.

Elizabeth looked Bobbi in the eye and briefly weighed her next words before speaking, "This might seem like a strange question," Bobbi visibly stiffened, and Elizabeth fleetingly wondered if it was because she was expecting a question she couldn't answer regarding her mother's test results or some sort of strange inquiry regarding her personally. Elizabeth smiled and continued in a lowered voice, "but, I'm just wondering if you could recommend a good place to hang out and meet interesting people." She raised her eyebrows to convey her meaning and Bobbi relaxed and mirrored Elizabeth's smile. "You see, I'm staying with my mother now, but I live in Boston."

Her smile widened and the tops of her ears turned pink. "Yea, sure...I think I know what you mean. There's a bar just off 82 called Luna's...Ladies nights are on Tuesdays and Thursdays. The rest of the week, it's mixed. My girlfriend and I are planning to go tomorrow with some of our friends if you're interested in joining us."

"Yea, I might." Elizabeth broke off as the door behind her began to open. Bobbi held up the folders, winked at Elizabeth and moved down the hallway. Patty looked at Elizabeth who couldn't hide the blush that was creeping up from her chest to her neck. The expression on Patty's face was the same one she used when Elizabeth was a child to let her know she knew something was up, but she wasn't going to pursue it right then.

~~~

"I'll just cut to the chase. This first round of chemo did very little to rid your body of the cancer. Your labs show that some of your levels are lower than we like to see, which means that your marrow is struggling to produce healthy cells. This isn't surprising given the type of cancer you have and the treatment you've already undergone. So, I'd like to get you a transfusion to help assuage that and build your blood back up some. We'll also need to get you on a schedule for more transfusions to keep your levels where we need them." Patty went stock still, and Dr. Martin just continued.

"As I indicated at the beginning, this happens more often than not; we're still very early in the process and there's still reason to hope. Usually what we do is make a few adjustments on levels and repeat the cycle. And if that doesn't do the trick, there are some other options that we can discuss at that time.

"Now as you already know, the previous round of chemo has hit your immune system pretty hard so you'll have to be even more careful during this second round and in the weeks and months that follow. You'll need to wear a mask out in public and limit your visitors to only healthy people to lower the risk of secondary infection."

Elizabeth was first to respond, she was barely able to contain her anger. "Just so we're clear here, Doc- I want to make sure I understand this correctly. The first round of chemo didn't work so now we have to do another round of the same thing, which didn't work...which will be worse this time because her system is compromised and the doses will be higher? And it still might not work? Isn't there something more or better we can do?" She let out a shuddering breath, and fought hard to keep herself from crying. Patty squeezed her hand in her own and looked expectantly at the doctor.

Dr. Martin nodded his understanding and remained calm, his voice still gentle. "I understand your frustration and disappointment; I know this is difficult to hear, I know it's hard to go through and I know how disheartening setbacks can be. Please know that we are and will continue to do everything we can to help you both through this, and after the next round of chemo there are some other options that we can explore. Some of those options are more invasive, there are some off label treatments as well as a couple clinical trials currently available that are showing some promising results. Some of the other treatment options are only appropriate after we've been able to kill most of the cancer cells...Have you done any research into this on the internet?" Both Patty and Elizabeth nodded and he continued. "Good. Are you aware of the Lymphoma and Leukemia Society?"

They both nodded and Elizabeth added, "I've looked at several different websites for information, but have so far kept it pretty limited to what Mom's going through. I read up on her specific type of cancer and a few articles pertaining to general treatment as well as a couple regarding her specific medications trying to get a better understanding of what other people have gone through, what we might expect, etc. I didn't get into many of the other treatment options because they didn't seem to apply at the time. Mom?"

"To be honest, I couldn't look at it for very long.

I have read all the information that you and the nurses have provided, but beyond that I just can't know it all. I still can't believe I have this disease."

"Patty, please don't take this the wrong way, but have you given any thought to talking to a counselor about it? We have some really good people and groups on staff that you both would probably benefit from, and having other people that can relate to what you're going through would probably help you deal with it better. There's a strong support network if you're interested. You don't have to go through this alone."

Patty just nodded at him and Elizabeth remained silent, giving thought to his suggestion.

"Elizabeth, it's good that you've looked into this stuff. Information is the best tool you can have and LLS.org is a great resource and a good organization. I'm glad that you are being proactive in that way, although I would caution you that each case is unique and people don't always react the same way to treatment. Cancer, even of the same type, doesn't always respond to treatment predictably because there are quite a few factors that have to be taken into account and some variables are completely unknown. Even in this day and age, with all the medical advancements we've been able to make, we still don't have a cure and the results of treatment remain uncertain, even if statistically predictable." He took a deep breath and clasped his fingers together in front of him on his desk in front of himself.

"Do you have any information on those groups you mentioned?"

Chapter 26

It was around 7pm and they were in the truck on their way home; they hardly spoke at all, both deep in thought. Patty scheduled herself an appointment with her dentist for the following day and let out a long breath in an effort to keep herself in check. Elizabeth knew this all must be the hardest thing Patty had ever lived through and often tried to put herself in Patty's shoes using what she knew about her mother to understand her better in this situation. As for what she herself was feeling, the word that readily came to mind was unraveled, but even that didn't touch it. Every day that she spent with her mother and this cancer she could feel the walls that she protected herself with, the strength she drew upon, the resolve and optimism she moved forward with disintegrating and becoming more like an eggshell than the iron clad brick she had always imagined. She needed to get away for a couple hours, get her head and her heart together and if that didn't work she needed to find a distraction. If even for a couple minutes she needed to feel something other than the lingering despair the situation shrouded her in.

"Mom, if you don't mind, I'm thinking that I need to get out for a couple hours and do some thinking."

"No, I don't mind, Ellie. It's been a long hard day and I'm kind of feeling like I want to be alone for a little while too. I was thinking that I'd just go to bed anyway. "

I don't want to be alone I just don't want to be here right now. "Ok then, I'll take care of Riley and grab a jacket and head out then- I'll probably be pretty late."

"I can take care of Riley, Honey. Don't worry about it…Other than my mood and being a little tired, I'm actually feeling alright- that transfusion must be helping…Maybe I'm part vampire." She giggled despite herself.

Elizabeth rolled her eyes, "You've been reading way too much Twilight." She chuckled, "I love you, Mom- You always know how to laugh." *I wish I had inherited that trait from you, Mom.*

~~~

An hour later, Elizabeth pulled the Chevy into the gravel drive and cut the engine. She sat there for a few minutes looking out the window at the house before her, the warm golden light filtered through the windows in the door and around the curtains, wondering if she'd lost her mind. Finally, she decided that it didn't matter and things were always better when she didn't think too hard about them. They were both adults and that afforded them certain freedoms. *Right?*

Shoving her reservations out of her mind, she grabbed a couple things out of her bag and shoved it under the seat, checked herself in the rearview mirror, grabbed the keys out of the ignition and got out of the truck. As she traversed the stone walkway, she noticed the lingering smell of grilling out mixed with new grass, pine and old leaves. She heard the faint sounds of a neighborhood settling down for the evening: a dog barking, it's owner calling it in, children's shrill little voices raised in excitement, a car door shutting. She straightened her shirt and fluffed her hair as she stepped up the three steps to the porch, noted the silhouettes of hanging planters along the top span along with a couple Adirondack chairs and a small table. She briefly wondered if his mother, Donna, had arranged it or whether he did it himself.

She reached out her finger, pressed it to the doorbell and turned to gaze out from the house, not really seeing anything much in the moonlight. Charlie opened the door, and the sounds of Ray LaMontagne drifted out.

"Hi Elle- oh man, I must have forgotten to turn the porch light on. Sorry about that." He smiled apologetically at her, his eyes sparkling, appraising her openly before he caught himself. She met his gaze with an amused one of her own and took in his disheveled appearance. His hair was damp and tousled, he was wearing a clean white tee-shirt, a pair of faded 501's and his feet were bare. His face was fresh looking and judging from the tiny tear of tissue on his neck he had recently shaved. They stood like that for a few seconds, her amusement deepening.

"Aren't you going to invite me in?" She asked playfully, a seductive smile on her lips. She stepped closer to Charlie and gently ran a finger across his chest, using the pressure to push him inside, stepping in after. He gasped in surprise and swung the door closed behind them.

He gulped. "I heard about your mom…"

"I don't want to talk about it." She inched closer, watched the pulse jumping in his neck. She could smell the fresh spicy scent of his aftershave and laid her hand flat on his chest running it up to his shoulder, watching the rise and fall of his breathing, the gooseflesh appearing on the skin she could see near his collar. She inched a bit closer to him still, his breath tickled her ear and she could feel him inhale deeply, undoubtedly taking her in. She ran her fingers to the nape of his neck, and up into the hair on the back of his head. He let out a shuddering breath, his control barely hanging by a thread.

She closed the gap between their bodies, "You smell good." She rubbed her cheek along his jaw and brought their faces together, just an inch apart.

"What are you doing?" His breathing was hard, his resolve in tatters. He placed his hands on her hips and she looked into the dark pools of his eyes, the blue of his irises a faint line around the dilation shouting his desire, matching her own.

"I think you know," she whispered and brought their mouths together, surprised at how soft his lips were. Distantly, she wondered how much softer Hailey's lips would be and quickly banished the thought. Their mouths pressed together and she opened slightly inviting him in. He tightened his grip on her hips and pressed their bodies together. Their tongues danced and explored each other until they were breathless, their chests heaving. Elizabeth was the first to pull away and Charlie staggered into the void she left. She grabbed his hand and pulled him into the living room.

He followed her to the couch, and pulled her in for another kiss, this time taking her face into his hands and claiming her lips with his own. She sighed and reached down to unbutton his jeans, feeling his flesh straining to be set free, pulling the fly open in one motion. She ran her fingers under the waistband and around to the seat where she cupped his firm ass before shoving his pants down. *No underwear? My my Charlie, seems like we are on the same page.*

He grabbed her hand and looked into her eyes.

"Are you sure?"

"Yes." He unzipped her hoodie and found the front of her shirt, fumbling with the small pearl buttons and straining to keep from ripping it open. She laughed and pushed him down onto the couch.

"Let me," she said as she shimmied out of the jacket and reached up to undo each button with a delicious slowness, breaking eye contact only long enough to glance down at him to confirm the level of his arousal. Charlie unconsciously licked his lips. "Take that off." She told him, nodding her head to indicate his shirt. In one smooth motion he leaned forward and removed his shirt, and then he kicked his jeans off. *My God he really is beautiful.*

She gazed down at him, noting his perfect chest, his broad shoulders and taut abs, his long lean muscles, the downy blond hair on his chest, getting darker as it trailed from his belly button down to lower places and getting lighter again as it covered his strong thighs and disappeared from view at the bend of his knees.

She spread her shirt open to reveal her breasts and he leaned forward reaching for her. "You're so beautiful," he murmured, his voice gruff. He took her into his hands squeezed her flesh, felt the weight of her, rubbed her nipples with his thumbs all the while watching the skin tighten and pucker, the nipples forming hard buds. She pulled something from her pocket, and placed a knee on either side of his legs, her skirt riding up her thighs with the motion. She grabbed his hair and kissed him again as he pushed her shirt off her shoulders, his kisses moved in a wet trail from her lips to her jaw to her neck to her collar bone to her shoulder. And she took the opportunity to open the condom wrapper in her hand. His fingers were gently tracing circles lower and lower down her back, around her ass and down her thigh where he tickled a line back up her inner thigh. "God you smell so good." He told her as he slowly teased her flesh, inching upward until he finally found her warm wet and waiting; his eyes were on her face and when she parted her lips in anticipation he kissed her. She let out a gasp as he ran his fingers along her wetness and brushed against her nerve center before sliding his hand back down her thigh. His breath was labored and she was having a hard time not fumbling the latex sheath in her hand.

"Here, let's put this on you before I drop it." She reached for him and ran a finger along his flesh, watching as he jerked and twitched. This made her smile. In one motion she placed the condom and gently rolled it down his length. He let out the breath he was holding and she lowered herself down onto him, letting him fill her up. In that moment there was nothing but his body inside hers, nothing but the blood rushing into her ears, the feeling of her sex and the friction of their motion, the feeling of her nails on his back, his teeth on her chest, the sounds of their grunts and sighs and moans and the building pressure of her eventual release.

She closed her eyes and when she came and it wasn't Charlie's face she saw. He was inside her, but he wasn't the one on her mind in that moment. This wasn't a shocking revelation for her; it wasn't even a mild surprise, but for some reason it wasn't exactly a welcome idea just then, either. It would be something she needed to think about, but later…much later.

After they had expressed their physical needs a few more times with each other, in various places along the path to the bedroom where they finally separated entirely sweaty and spent and their chests heaving Charlie rolled over on his side and looked at Elizabeth.

"Does she know how you feel about her?" He asked with no judgment, no reproach, just a simple honest question.

"What are you talking about?" *Oh my God. What is he talking about?*

"The woman whose name you called out the first time you climaxed out on the couch and then whispered when I had my mouth on you. Have you told her how you feel about her?" His eyes and smile were kind and gentle and he reached out a hand to move her hair from her forehead.

Shit damn motherfucker. I can't get out of this with a lie, not with Charlie. He must have seen panic in her eyes because he continued, "I don't mind getting used by a beautiful, smoking hot woman who just wants to numb some pain or fill a gap- I can even play surrogate for you– I honestly don't mind." *Goddamned it why does he have to be so sweet?* "In fact, I've got someone else in my heart too, so I'm not innocent, but I am also your friend – at least I would hope so." He tilted her chin so that their eyes met. "You can talk to me Elle. I'm not going to turn you away for anything. You can have any part of my body any time you want or need it, whether it's my ear or my shoulder or…well, you know. I'm here for you."

She started to cry and he gathered her up into his arms and held her there for a while, murmuring reassurances and laying soft kisses into her hair. When her sobs finally stopped, she told him everything. They talked well into the wee hours and shared intimate details of their lives, their fears, hopes, desires. It felt good to get it out there, to purge everything that had been such a heavy weight. Charlie was kind and understanding and listened intently, offering encouragement and his thoughts when it seemed appropriate, sharing his own stories or take on things. As the night went on Elizabeth felt something shift inside herself, a feeling of calm and resolve that hadn't been there before.

"Thank you Charlie, for everything," she said as she gathered up her jacket and keys. "You know, I'm really glad we ran into each other. Why don't we go out one of these nights and do something?"

He smiled at her, "I'd like that, Elle. Can I call you?"

"Of course, that is why I gave you my number, after all." She paused and added, "And until we get our shit straightened out with our other people, I wouldn't mind repeating last night- if you're game."

"Oh, I'm always game – but that ball's in your court." She nodded and smiled, waved a hand at him as she made her way down the walkway to the red Chevy truck. "Hey, Elizabeth?"

"Yea?"

"If she doesn't know how lucky she is, she doesn't deserve you."

"It's the same for you, Charlie. And don't you forget it."

Chapter 27

"I didn't hear you come home last night – did you have a good time?" Patty sat in her favorite chair enjoying the morning sun coming through the window. She raised a mug of hot tea to her lips as she gently blew away some of the heat from that first sip. She looked at her daughter, trying to find any sign of what she'd been up to the night before. A shower and a few hours sleep couldn't erase the warm glow of her skin or the smile that played on her lips, the spring in her step or the fact that she was actually humming. Patty raised an eyebrow, "It would appear so," she said and smiled at Elizabeth knowingly.

"I don't know what you're talking about, Mom," she said with a wide grin on her face as she bent down to place a kiss on her mother's cheek. "Good morning. How did you sleep?" She sat down on the couch and began eating the bowl of cereal she had brought with her.

"Not quite as well as you, it would seem. I hope you were careful." She took a sip of her tea to hide her face. "Was it that Bobbi woman we met at the hospital?"

Elizabeth nearly choked on her bite, barely getting it swallowed before it spewed back into the bowl, her eyes wide as saucers. "MOM!"

Patty was laughing now. "What? Can't a mother be concerned for the well being of her adult daughter?" She emphasized 'adult' for effect. "We may not be up in each other's business, but it's not like we've never talked about this stuff before, Ellie.

Besides, ever since you were in college I've known more about that side of your life than I ever thought I would want to - Derek, Jamie, Jennifer, Brandon, Troy, Kristen." Elizabeth looked at her mother in near shock. *What?!* "Of course I knew about them, Elizabeth. I'm you're mother, and I know you. You acted differently around them, talked about them differently, looked at them differently from your regular friends when you brought some of them home on breaks. And, for your information, the walls here are not that thick. That's how I knew about Jennifer." She looked pointedly at Elizabeth. *Oh my God, this isn't happening.* "The point is, you're a grown woman and I respect that. I've raised you from a tiny helpless baby into a wonderful, warm, generous, smart, beautiful, talented and successful woman and I love you with all my heart. I'm glad that you're putting yourself out there, but I do wish you'd find love, Honey."

Elizabeth took her mirth as a good sign and decided to change the subject. "You seem to be feeling better today, even some of your color has returned."

"Like I said last night, I must be part vampire- I've certainly been feeling a bit undead lately. I'm definitely not even close to 100%, but I did get a good night's sleep and I'm not as weak this morning." She took another sip of her tea and watched her daughter over the rim of her cup.

Elizabeth pulled her feet up underneath her. "If you must know, I went to see Charlie Moore last night." Patty raised her eyebrows and Elizabeth quickly added, "He's just a friend. Anyway, we stayed up until the wee hours talking," *There, not a complete lie. Mom doesn't need to know everything.* She smiled to herself. "And it was great. He's grown into such a nice guy. Who would have thought that gangly awkward kid with the acne and the headgear would have become such an attractive and successful veterinarian? Did you hear about Bill falling off the barn roof a few weeks ago?"

Patty shook her head, "Been kind of out of the loop."

"Yea I guess so, sorry Mom. So, yea I guess he broke his leg and cracked a couple vertebra; he's been laid up ever since." Elizabeth went on to tell Patty a few other pieces of town gossip that Charlie told her and Patty seemed to be satisfied with this. Elizabeth was certain that Patty knew the score there, but was relieved when she didn't push the issue any further.

"Oh, before I forget. Hailey is coming over later." Her eyes were trained on Elizabeth, who tried not to squirm under the scrutiny.

Chapter 28

A wintery mix was coming down and had been for a while when they were finally on their way home from the dentist's office and the other errands they had run that day. Elizabeth took some time to handle a couple phone calls and emails for work while Patty learned all about periodontal disease and its treatment.

Afterward, they stopped by the bakery to check on business and pick up a few things. Patty asked Jake to send someone over to the Moore place with some deli items, bread and a pie with a message for Bill to 'get well soon.' From there they went to the grocery store and bought some stuff to carry them through the next few days. When they got home, Patty let Riley out while Elizabeth carried their stuff in to the kitchen and put it away.

"Hey Mom? It's pretty cold in here, what do you say I make a fire and some hot cocoa?"

"That sounds like a great idea, Ellie. Why don't I get the cocoa started while you do the fire?" She had already gotten a saucepan out of the cupboard and was getting the milk out of the fridge.

"Alright, it's a deal." She gave Patty a wide grin and went out onto the back porch to gather enough firewood for the night. She put all but one piece of the wood into the rack and grabbed the hatchet to cut some kindling. Once she had enough, she started stacking the logs and kindling and wadded up paper and lit it. The logs caught fairly quickly and she adjusted the flue to let the smoke out, replaced the fire screen and headed back toward the kitchen.

"Oh man, I love a good fire," she said as she rounded the corner. Patty was at the counter chopping a mixture of milk and dark chocolates to stir into the warmed milk.

"Me too. I love the smell they give to fall and winter, I love the crackling sound they make, and I even love how you have to slowly spin like you're on a rotisserie when you stand close after coming in from the cold. It's just such a primitive and perfect thing…Can you reach into that cabinet and pull out the marshmallows please?"

"Sure, Mom. I'll grab some mugs too."

Just then the phone rang and there was a knock on the door. Elizabeth held up her hand to her mom and started toward the phone. She called out to the door "Be right there! Hello? Hi Donna, yes she's right here." She handed the phone to her mom who had just put the chocolate into the heated milk and was stirring it. 'Thank you' she mouthed "Hi Donna…"

Elizabeth went to answer the door where Riley was already waiting with his tail wagging to find Hailey shivering and wet, her hair plastered to her head and her pant legs soaked from the thighs down. "Suddenly the sky opened up," she said with sparkling eyes and a devilish grin.

"Oh no! Hailey! Come in come in – Why didn't you just get inside? You don't have to wait on the porch like everyone else." Elizabeth ushered Hailey inside and took the canvas bag from her and sat it on the floor and moved to help Hailey out of her backpack and jacket. "Here, let me help you with that."

"Thanks. Man I didn't expect that – one second it was barely drizzling and then next second it was dropping buckets. It even went down my back."

"Well, why don't we get you out of these wet clothes and you can borrow some of mine while we put these in the dryer?" Unconsciously Hailey raised an eyebrow, and the idea of getting Hailey out of her clothes made Elizabeth blush. Inwardly she was mad at herself for it. *Oh yea, that's real smooth, Elle. Blushing like a schoolgirl. Geez.*

"Let's just take this into the kitchen and we'll go get you all fixed up." She picked up the canvas bag and Hailey grabbed her backpack. When they entered the kitchen they were greeted by Patty and steaming mugs of hot chocolate.

"Look who's here"

Patty's eyes were wide with surprise at Hailey's appearance. "Hailey! What happened?"

Hailey shrugged and set her bag down on one of the barstools. "It decided to pour. Oh my God, is that hot chocolate?" Patty smiled and handed them each a mug of the steaming liquid. Hailey smiled appreciatively and took a sip. "Oh that's perfect, thank you."

"Mom, I'm going to take Hailey and get her a towel and some dry clothes. We'll be back in a minute." Elizabeth grabbed Hailey's hand and pulled her to the back of the house where her room was. "Come on, we'll get you warmed up in no time." Hailey arched an eyebrow and followed along.

A few steps down the hallway Elizabeth turned to Hailey and caught her checking her out. Hailey raised her eyes to Elizabeth's and for a second Elizabeth thought she saw a flash of something there. She smiled and gestured to a door, "There are towels in this closet here if you want to grab one. And the laundry room's just through there. I'll just see if I can find you something to wear. You can use my room."

Hailey grabbed a towel from the linen closet and started drying her hair as she followed Elizabeth into her room. "Wow, look at this room – it's like a blast from the past, huh?" She looked at the stuff on the shelves and walls, all pieces of Elizabeth's youth- awards and trophies, books, pictures, nick-knacks and such.

"Yea, I've got a lot of memories here. I've told Mom that I'd help her box all this stuff up if she wanted to use this room, but she refuses. I have to admit that it is pretty cool to come home and have this place, kind of like a vault, you know? Makes it harder to forget the good times along with the rest, I guess."

"Yea." Hailey's expression was wistful. "My childhood room in California is kind of like a shrine to someone else," she said almost to herself.

Elizabeth wasn't sure she should press the issue, so she just looked up at Hailey and let her decide whether she wanted to continue. When she didn't, Elizabeth said, "I hope you don't mind sweats. These should be comfortable and warm. And there are some thick socks that should help too. Elizabeth gestured to the bed where she'd laid a pair of well loved sweatpants that had 'TARHEELS' down the left leg and an equally adored navy blue zip up hoodie along with a white tee shirt and a pair of socks.

Hailey set the towel on the chair, pulled her hair back into a messy pony tail and took off her wet shirt. She started to peel her pants off revealing more of her flawless white skin. For a second Elizabeth couldn't breathe and she felt her blood pooling places not her brain. "Well ok then," she said as she quickly looked away. "I'll just let you get changed." And she rushed out the door and down the hall to the kitchen. "Hey Mom, has Riley been out recently?"

"Yes, I let him out a few minutes ago; he's in here drying off near the fire."

"Alright- do you want me to start dinner?"

"Only if you're hungry, Sweetheart. It won't take long to heat up stew."

Oh I'm hungry, but it's not stew I want. "Well I guess I'll wait for Hailey then."

"Wait for me for what? Here's your hot chocolate. Thanks for the clothes." She smiled as she handed Elizabeth her abandoned mug and their fingers brushed. Elizabeth felt her ears go hot and was thankful that her hair was down to cover the red that was surely there.

"Thanks. I was just wondering if I should heat dinner now or wait." *Damn she looks good in my clothes…almost as good as she looked out of them.*

"Either way is fine by me. If you're hungry now I could eat. I brought some stuff with me too." She pulled up her canvas sack and started pulling stuff from it. "Let's see…we've got some cheeses, some chocolate covered native berries and some wine that I got while I was in Oregon…some popcorn…I also brought a couple movies. I thought with the weather it might be nice to huddle under blankets eat popcorn and do something mindless…if you're interested."

"That sounds great, Hailey. We're having vegetable stew and sourdough rolls for dinner. Sounds like it will all go nicely together." She pulled a half gallon container of stew from the bakery out of the fridge and poured it into the saucepan waiting on the range.

"Do you need any help?" Hailey said from just inches over her shoulder, which made Elizabeth jump. *How does she do that?*

"You seem to have a way with sneaking up on me." She smiled. "No, this won't take much to do, but thank you. Why don't you go visit with Mom and I'll bring it out when it's done."

"If you're sure?"

"Yep- it's no problem." She smiled and pulled three bowls and three spoons out and grabbed a tray from another cabinet and continued to get dinner ready.

They ate in the living room while they got caught up on the last few days. Hailey told them all about her trip to Oregon, Patty told her about the doctor and dentist visits, Elizabeth mostly listened and watched Hailey, trying not to be obvious about it.

The bowls were taken to the kitchen and Hailey let the others decide which movie to start with while she made 3 bags of microwave popcorn. When she returned to the living room, they had decided to watch 'Limitless' with Bradley Cooper and Robert DeNiro. Patty started dozing near the end and once it was over she told the girls goodnight, reminded Elizabeth she thought they should leave around 10 in the morning and went to bed.

"Did you want to watch the other one?" Elizabeth asked Hailey, hopeful, not wanting the night to end just yet.

"Sure, if you want to- I know you have a long day tomorrow." She looked a bit sad, as if she regretted the reminder or thought maybe Elizabeth was just being polite.

"That's true, but I'm not eager to get it started right away. Stay, we'll watch this." She placed her hand on Hailey's arm. "Please?"

"Ok – you set it up and I'll get us something to drink – oh! And we've still got those chocolate berries I brought. Would you like some?"

"Yea, that sounds great. Would you mind bringing me one of those orange sodas from the fridge?" "Sure thing."

They got themselves situated on the sectional; Hailey nestled in the corner along the wide chaise and Elizabeth sat next to her sharing a heavy oversized quilt, her socked feet tucked up underneath her. Elizabeth was amazed at how sweet the chocolate covered berries were and Hailey briefly explained that it was because of Oregon's moderate climate with a long spring and early summer, lots of rain. Once the film began, they didn't say much.

A few hours later Elizabeth opened her eyes and felt Hailey's steady breath in her hair. She carefully tilted her head to see better in the blue glow from the TV and realized that she had her head on Hailey's breast, her arm was around her waist, her leg was draped over Hailey's legs and Hailey had her arm around Elizabeth's middle. The side pillows from the couch had been kicked off in an unconscious effort to make more room and Hailey was sleeping deeply. Elizabeth sighed and shifted slightly. At the movement, Hailey rolled toward her, bringing her leg up to rest between Elizabeth's thighs and tightened her grip pulling Elizabeth in even closer. *Oh God.* It had been a very long time since she wanted to actually sleep with someone, and this felt good. Usually when she woke up like this, she couldn't get out of there fast enough, but somehow Hailey broke past her defenses and she couldn't fight it anymore, didn't want to. Maybe in the light of day things would look differently, but right then this was exactly where she wanted to be. She sighed deeply and let herself drift back off to sleep.

~~~

The day was dawning and the morning sun had just begun to illuminate the sky when Hailey opened her eyes. She was holding someone in her arms, her front to their back and as she followed the sensation down her arm to her hand she realized she was holding a breast. She tightened her arm and gently squeezed her hand then stopped abruptly.

It had taken her a moment to realize where she was and when she did it was with a start. She made a move to get up but Elizabeth stopped her. "You don't have to go," she said softly.

Elizabeth turned to face Hailey and looked into her eyes. She saw the desire there and also the fear. Then she focused on her lips.

"Elizabeth, I..." She didn't give her a chance to finish that thought; instead she closed the gap between them and brushed her lips against Hailey's. Gently at first, then when Hailey didn't stop her, she added a tiny bit more pressure, thrilling at how soft they were. Soon Hailey was responding and the kiss between them grew until they were nearly devoured by it and the grabbing and groping that accompanied it. Suddenly Hailey pushed against Elizabeth and broke the contact, their chests heaving and she practically jumped off the couch. "I can't do this, Elizabeth. I'm sorry...I...just can't." She practically ran out of the house leaving a breathless Elizabeth stunned and confused. *Well that didn't go the way I dreamed it.*

Chapter 29

When they entered the treatment area Patty was met with various greetings and several smiling faces. June hooked her up to the drip line and covered her with a couple blankets to help keep her warm.

"You don't have to stay here with me for this, Ellie. I'm thinking that I might try to sleep anyway- why don't you go on and do what you need to do. I'll be alright here." Her eyes were tired and a little sad, but she nodded in encouragement toward Elizabeth and then to the exit.

"Are you sure, Mom? I don't need to go anywhere, there's nothing I need to do right now...I don't want to leave you alone." The concern was evident in her voice and in her wringing hands.

"I'm sure, Sweetheart. I didn't sleep much last night and I'm truly tired. This is going to take a few hours- you don't need to be here to watch me sleep." She grabbed Elizabeth's hand and gave it a squeeze, then closed her eyes.

"Ok, Mom – I'll be nearby if you need me and I'll come check on you in a couple hours. I love you."

"I love you too, Sweetie. Now go. Have a day."

Elizabeth wandered over to the nurses' station, pulling out a pamphlet touting the MCMC facilities from her back pocket. "Can you tell me where this is?" She held up the paper to one of the nurses and pointed to a photograph of an atrium. "Oh, it's you." She smiled.

"Hey there – Elizabeth, right?" Bobbi was

wearing black scrubs covered in red and green chili peppers. "Didn't see you at Luna's the other night." It was equal parts question and statement, her Honey eyes sparkling.

"Yea, we ended up having company instead. Are you guys going again soon?"

"It can be arranged…why don't I give you my number and you can text if you're heading out…if you want. It might take a little bit for my girlfriend to arrange things at home- she's got kids- but I'm always free and she can join us when she gets there." She pulled a scrap of paper and pen from the desk and began to write down her information.

"Cool. If I can get away I'll let you know. It would be good to get out and have some fun." Immediately she felt intensely guilty and selfish knowing that her mother couldn't do anything differently and probably wished she could have more fun too. She looked in the direction that she had come from and saw her mother reclined in the chair, hardly moved from when she left her. *Who the hell am I to have any kind of life now when she might not even live? Haven't I left her alone enough already? Granted, it wasn't while she was getting chemo, but still- she needs me. I can't just go off like that all the time.*

She pulled herself back together, rubbed hard at her forehead and looked apologetically at Bobbi who was looking at her with a look of kind concern.

"It's ok, you know." She told her in a soft voice.

"What's ok?" She asked, confused by the seemingly random statement.

"Everything you're feeling- all the conflicting emotions, the guilt, the fear, the anger…you're entitled to feel each and every one, but it's also ok to feel some happiness and hope when you can. It's not something you need to apologize for."

She only nodded.

Bobbi looked at the photo that Elizabeth had asked about and gave her directions.

"I hope we see you soon, it would do you good. And that would mean that things are ok, right?"

"I hope so. Thanks." She walked in the direction that Bobbi had pointed.

~~~

Elizabeth returned to the treatment room to find Patty awake and staring blindly out the window. Her skin was pallid and her expression was lax.

"Hey Mom." Elizabeth moved one of the chairs so that she could better see Patty's face. She reached out and placed her hand on Patty's, it was cold.

"Hi Ellie." Her voice was barely audible.

"How are you doing?" Elizabeth knew it was a stupid question; it was obvious that her mother was not doing well. Not for the first time Elizabeth noticed how thin and pale her mother was and her heart wrenched for the pain she must be going through.

"I want to go home."

"It looks like the bag's almost empty, Mom…we'll be heading home soon. Can I get you something while we wait? Some more water? A magazine?"

"No. I just want to go home." She closed her eyes and stayed silent for the remainder of her treatment. Bobbi unhooked the bag and cleaned the port and did everything else that would allow them to get on their way. They rode in silence, Elizabeth's face grim, Patty's streaked with tears.

Chapter 30

"Peta, I think I'm in trouble and I need some advice."

"What kind of trouble? You didn't get arrested did you?" Peter's voice was full of concern.

Hailey chuckled softly and walked across her living room and looked out the window. The new growth on the trees was highlighted by the afternoon sun. She chuckled, "No, no. I didn't get arrested. It's nothing like that."

"Ok, phew. I thought maybe you got caught with your pants down having a little fun time with the Sherriff's daughter or some such thing." Peter said with a laugh.

"What!? When have I ever gotten caught with my pants down? Wait, don't answer that." She laughed.

"Well, there was that little stunt there in your early 20's with, what was her name? Britney? Heather?"

"Kayla. Oh man, the look on her mother's face!" She was near tears laughing so hard. "She kept screaming 'It's a girl! It's a girl!' I didn't know whether to run or hand her a cigar and congratulate her."

"Oh man, those were some fun times…I wonder whatever happened to her?"

"Last I heard she married that marine biology student she was cheating on with me and they moved to New Zealand to do research."

"Yea, I think I remember that now." He cleared his throat and it sounded like he took a sip of something. "So who is she?"

"Who's who?"

"Don't play dumb with me, Hailey Claire Jensen. You called me, remember? Who's the woman that's got you tied in knots so bad you had to call me for advice?"

"How do you know it's a woman?" She replied with an indignant tone.

"Wishful thinking, maybe?"

She let out a heavy sigh and started playing with the strings fringing her cutoff shorts. "It's Elizabeth Thornton." She let that sink in for a few moments.

"THE Elizabeth Thornton? Patty's daughter, Elizabeth Thornton? The one you told me about? The one you've been mooning over for weeks now? I thought she was straight? Ok. Spill it."

"She kissed me."

"She kissed you? Like, how? A peck on the cheek or like a real kiss? How did it happen? Where were you? Did you kiss her back? I need details!"

"A real full on with tongue kiss complete with heavy petting and of course I kissed her back." She continued to tell Peter the whole story beginning the night before and ending with her running out of the house like her ass was on fire.

"Wow, you made out with her. It was a good, though?"

"I know. And yea, it was toes curling heart hammering breath stuck amazing." Her lips tingled at the memory of it and her heart was again jack hammering in her chest.

"So it seems like she's not totally straight…that's good, right? I guess I don't understand what the problem is."

"Well for one, 'not totally straight' is still a little straight and you remember Kayla. And Madyson. And Jenna. When things got a little too real, they went running back to the dark side. Then there's the whole issue of her mom having cancer and maybe dying. What if this is all just some sort of distraction for her? What if with everything she's going through with Patty she's just confused? And then, there's the issue of her living all the way in Boston. When this thing with Patty is finished, she's going to go back there, and where does that leave me?" She put her head back on the couch and pinched the bridge of her nose.

Peter took another sip from his drink and Hailey could hear the sliding of a glass door open and close. "Oh Honey. You really like her, don't you?"

"Yea. I do, Peta. Given half a chance I could fall in love with her." She let out a long sigh, knowing that she was already well on her way and there was nothing she could do to stop it. Not if she was being honest with herself. "What am I gonna do?"

"Damn." He weighed his next words for what seemed to Hailey like an eternity. "You know I love you, right?"

"You know I hate it when you feel you have to remind me of that fact before you tell me something you think I'm going to find hard to hear, right?" The words came out a little more harshly than the light tone she was going for and she sighed and spoke softly. "I called you because I *want* to hear what you're going to tell me, Peta. Maybe because even I know I *need* to hear it."

"Ok, then. Here goes." He took another sip and

said, "You can't keep your heart locked away forever, Hailey. I know it's been hard for you- harder than it is for most, probably. I know because I was there with you. After your mother left you were so angry. I remember spending quite a few of those first nights crying to Mom wondering why you didn't like me. Wondering what I did to make you so mad." His voice softened, "but she explained it to me and you came around, eventually."

Hailey choked back a sob. "I never knew."

"And when Nonna died it wrecked us both. She was as much a friend to me as she was to you. We were there for each other then, but it still wasn't easy. And then a few years later your father had his heart attack. It was devastating, and you retreated back into yourself. You had spent your whole life trying to live up to his image of you and when he was gone it was like you didn't know who to be. I was afraid I'd never see you happy again. Add to that all the women who didn't last for whatever reasons, Genevieve was just the icing on that cake. I know. Life's like that, you know? It's hard. But you keep on living, right?"

Hailey's tears were running full stream now and she had to blow her nose.

"That's the thing about death and love Hailey. They never happen when it's convenient. But as long as you're alive you have to keep on living and as long as there's love in your heart you have to share it. You are such a wonderful woman, Hails. I hate for you not to share yourself just because you're afraid to get hurt again."

"I know. Me too, Peter." *Me too.*

Chapter 31

Thursday morning began earlier than normal with the sounds of Patty barking out a cough that sounded like a beach full of seals. Elizabeth stumbled to her room still half asleep and opened the door to find Patty soaked with sweat and out of breath; her face was red with the strain of coughing. Elizabeth touched the back of her hand to Patty's forehead and cheek and flinched.

"Oh my God, Mom – you're burning up. How long has this been going on?"

"Well, the coughing started about an hour ago…" More coughing.

"Let me get you some water." She grabbed the empty glass of the bedside table and took it to the bathroom. She returned with a full glass and a wet washcloth a minute later. "Here, have some of this."

Patty gulped down some of the water and laid back on her pillow to catch her breath. She looked her thanks to Elizabeth and placed the washcloth on her forehead.

"So the coughing started about an hour ago?"

"Yea, and with everything that this round of chemo is doing to me I wouldn't know when I started feeling sick, so don't ask."

"Ok well, let's you cleaned up and dressed. We'll go in a bit earlier today and maybe they can see you and get this figured out. We can't have you sick on top of being sick."

Elizabeth helped Patty out of bed and Patty

leaned heavily on her as they walked into the bathroom. It had been a long few days and nights for both women. Patty was much sicker this round than the last, spending a great deal of time fighting nausea and exhaustion and the other effects of the chemo. When she wasn't fighting it, she was sleeping, too weak and too tired to do much else and when they had to go back to the hospital for the next treatment, Elizabeth had to practically carry her.

Patty was so weak and sick in fact, that Elizabeth had to help her to shower; so during one of Patty's naps, Elizabeth went into town to a bed and bath store and bought a shower stool and a hand-shower attachment to make bathing easier for Patty. Not that needing help bathing was ever easy, but they both handled it with as much aplomb as they could muster.

They arrived at the hospital and pulled into the side lot. Elizabeth supported Patty through the side entrance that was reserved for cancer patients. Using this door was supposed to reduce Patty's exposure to germs, but despite this and the mask she wore everywhere she went – which was pretty much nowhere these days- she still caught something if her cough and fever were any indication. June came out from behind the nurses' station when she saw them approaching and helped Patty into one of the wheelchairs they kept nearby.

"Hi Patty. You don't look so good. Can you tell me what's going on?" June grabbed the wheelchair by the handles and was pushing Patty down the hall into one of the examination areas, Elizabeth following their heels. Patty started coughing again, so Elizabeth answered for her as they helped Patty onto the gurney.

"She's been coughing off and on like this for at least a couple hours now and has had a fever since before I checked on her this morning. She told me that she wouldn't know when she started feeling down from whatever she's caught because the chemo had her so low to begin with."

"Alright. Well with chemo it's not uncommon to get secondary infections and additional illness due to the compromised immune system...Alright, Patty can you hold this under your tongue please?" She placed a thermometer in Patty's mouth and began to check her blood pressure. "Ok, did you give her any Tylenol or Motrin to reduce the fever?"

"No – we didn't want to cause a weird reaction with all her other drugs and just came in here as soon as possible." Elizabeth was wringing her hands in concern, June nodded acknowledgement.

"Alright, blood pressure's a little higher than normal – let's see...102.1. Alright, well it's definitely a fever, but it's not that bad yet. I'll need you to disrobe and put this on, opening in the back." June handed Patty a blue cotton hospital gown. If you'll excuse me for a moment, I'll get Dr. Martin." June stood and exited the examination cubicle.

With the help of Elizabeth, Patty changed into the robe and laid back on the gurney. She closed her eyes as they waited and Elizabeth paced the length of the area back and forth. "You're gonna wear a rut in the floor if you keep pacing like that, Ellie. Why don't you pull up a chair and settle down some?"

"I know Mom, I'm sorry- I'm just so worried about you, you know? I don't know what else to do with myself." Elizabeth's voice broke and she was trying to control the sobs. The tears weren't so cooperative.

"I know Sweetie…I'm scared too."

The curtain slid to the side and Dr. Martin entered the area. "Good morning, sorry to keep you waiting." He smiled a gentle smile and acknowledged Patty and Elizabeth with a nod before turning his attention to the chart in his hand. "Looks like you have a fever and some coughing…have you noticed anything else new in the last couple days?" He looked at Patty for an answer.

"It's pretty hard to tell, Doc. This round of chemo has me feeling like I've been repeatedly hit by a truck." Her tone was humorless.

"Yes, that's understandable; I wish it weren't so. Well, let's have a look at you." Over the next several minutes, he asked questions while he conducted a thorough examination, looking in her ears and eyes and mouth and up her nose, listening to her breathing and heart, palpating her abdomen and lymph nodes, examining her tender skin for any rashes or abnormalities, especially around the site of the catheter, checking reflexes and so on. "Well, based on your symptoms I'm concluding that you have an upper respiratory infection; blood tests will give us a more concrete answer and I'd like to get you in for a couple chest x-rays to rule out something more subversive. Besides the cough you seem to have a slight rattle in your bronchia. It's early now, but it could very easy become pneumonia so I'd like to keep you here at the hospital so we can stay on top of it and prevent any further infections. I'll be prescribing an additional antibiotic and we'll be monitoring your fever. I want to see if we can use it to our advantage and have it help us kill this bug you seem to have, but if it gets too high we'll need to bring it down." Both Patty and Elizabeth's face drained of color.

"She needs to be hospitalized?" her eyes were wide.

"Yes." He looked at Patty. "I think it's best for you to remain in our care for the duration of this round of chemo and sometime after the course concludes so that we can stay on top of your progress and best care for you. I'm thinking that if everything goes well you'll be out of here in around 6 weeks. It might be a bit longer." He turned his attention to Elizabeth, "We'll have to keep her in a private room to minimize exposure to strangers and their germs; you'll have 24 hour access to her. I'll go get the admittance forms now."

Elizabeth's knees nearly gave out and she finally took a seat in the chair. All they could do was nod.

Once Patty was settled into her room and hooked up to the days' bags and monitors, she and Elizabeth made a list of the few things that might make the stay a bit more bearable. Elizabeth took the truck and went back home to make a few phone calls and pack a couple bags. She gathered some books, DVDs, some music, a deck of cards, lotion and toiletries and other necessaries that Patty might need or want in the next several days figuring she could always bring something more later. She checked the mail, let Riley out, showered and changed her clothes and returned to the hospital. By the time she got there it was well into the afternoon, and Patty was finished with her chemo treatment for the day.

"Hey Mom. How's it going?" She picked up the

empty cup and poured more water into it. Patty opened her eyes and offered a wan smile in answer. "That bad, huh? Can I get you anything, are you comfortable?"

"I'm a little cold."

After Elizabeth pulled down a couple blankets from the closet and draped them over Patty they exchanged strained bits of small talk. Elizabeth was too overwhelmed to talk about much and Patty was simply too sick and too tired; it was all starting to hit her hard and she needed time to herself to think and feel the boiling mix of things bubbling up within her. She was upset and angry and tired and sick and scared and as much as she loved Elizabeth she just wanted to be alone. Eventually Patty said as much to Elizabeth, and while she was a little hurt by her mother's obvious rejection of her company she reluctantly left promising she'd be back early in the morning.

When Elizabeth got home she let Riley out and as she sat on the step watching him run around the yard she let her tears flow freely. Sensing that something was wrong, Riley approached her carefully and began to give her tentative kisses on her face. Pretty soon Elizabeth was laughing and wiping at her face and Riley was acting a fool trying to get her to throw his ball for him. So she did until they were both tired.

She took Riley back into the house where he flopped unceremoniously onto the floor, his long pink tongue lolling out of his mouth. She put some food out for him, refilled his water, and took another shower in an attempt to wash the day away. She thought about calling Charlie but shook that thought away, opting to check out Luna's instead.

Chapter 32

"Hey Elizabeth over here!" Bobbi saw Elizabeth enter the bar and waved, calling to her from the table where she and her friends were having beers after work. Elizabeth saw the group and smiled gesturing with her hand to indicate she'd get a drink and be right over.

Luna's was almost packed which Elizabeth was surprised at. The crowd was nearly all women and the few men that were there seemed more interested in each other than in any of the ladies. Aside from the various neon beer signs, the interior was done in a rustic lodge style, all stripped timber columns and beams, rough hewn paneling, and wide panel floors. In the back there were 4 brightly lit pool tables and along one wall there were dart boards, a video golf game and an older version of Big Game Hunter.

An old jukebox sat lonely in a corner near a deejay booth that overlooked a small dance floor where several couples were moving to a Tegan and Sara remix. A 4 foot by 10 foot mirror hung on the wall behind the bar, adorned with various photographs and postcards from patrons' travels over the years.

As the crowd around the bar moved off, the bartender gave her an appraising look and smiled. She was a stocky 5'5" and looked to be about fifty with short spiky salt and pepper hair and skin that would have benefitted from more sun block in her youth. She wasn't unattractive with her square jaw and warm brown eyes.

"What can I do for you?" She drawled as she leaned on the bar.

"How about a hefeweizen and a tab," she said handing the bartender her I.D. and a credit card.

"Sure thing." She placed a curvy glass under the spigot and pulled the tap, filling the glass and then letting it settle before topping it off with a slice of lemon. "Here you go." She placed the full glass on the bar in front of Elizabeth and winked. "I'm Marty. If you need anything just let me know."

"Nice to meet you Marty." She stuck out her hand for Marty to shake it, which she did, holding onto it a second longer than normal. "I'm Elizabeth." Marty nodded and turned to help another customer down the bar and Elizabeth turned toward Bobbi and her friends.

"Hey. I was wondering if you were going to make it tonight." Bobbi stood on the foot rail of her stool and gave Elizabeth a brief greeting hug and kept her arm over Elizabeth's shoulder as she introduced her around the table. "Everyone, this is Elizabeth Thornton. This is Carey, Anne, Michelle, Jody and Hannah. Shelly should be arriving soon."

They all greeted her cheerfully and the perky brunette Hannah indicated an empty seat next to her. "You can sit here if you want – it's a good spot to people watch and I won't bite. Maybe." Hannah wiggled her eyebrows and Elizabeth laughed and sat down on the offered stool and looked out over the crowded bar.

"So how do you know our Bobbi?" This from the curvy Latina Michelle who was obviously with the huskier Jody, their hands were entwined and Jody had her arm wrapped around Michelle's waist.

"My mother's a patient at MCMC." She replied simply and took a sip of her beer not offering details.

They all just nodded as if that were explanation enough.

"So I haven't seen you here before...Do you live nearby?" This from Hannah who wore a mischievous grin.

"Well, I'm staying at my mom's house in Carbondale for now but I live in Boston now." She took another sip of her beer and rotated the glass on the table with her fingertips.

"Hey, there's Shelly." Bobbi got up and headed toward the entrance.

"Oh my fucking God, you have got to be shitting me." The whole table stared at Elizabeth in varying degrees of shock as Elizabeth smiled wide and stood up, moving around the table. "Shelly fucking Moore?! Are you serious?"

"Oh my God! Elle- what the hell are you doing here?" They practically leapt into each other's arms, a rush of laughs and excited exclamations. "I heard about your mom. If there's anything I can do..." She said it low so only Elizabeth could hear and squeezed her tighter.

Bobbi and the rest of the gang just watched the reunion with various expressions of amusement and concern.

"I take it you two know each other?" Bobbi said waving her beer at their hands still clasped together, fighting a wave of jealousy.

Shelly blushed and looked sideways at Elizabeth with a grin. "Elizabeth was my first crush- I mean bff in school."

Elizabeth playfully punched her in the arm, "What?! You never told me that! Man, high school would have been so much more interesting if you had." She wiggled her eyebrows suggestively and they both laughed. Bobbi's expression turned grim.

"Oh Baby, it's not like that," she said releasing Elizabeth's hand and kissing Bobbi soundly. "I'm madly in love with you." She smiled like the cat that ate the canary and turned to Elizabeth, "So, I hear you've been hanging out with my brother."

Elizabeth was surprised and didn't know whether to be angry at Charlie or embarrassed; either way she could feel the blush creeping up her neck. Shelly's eyebrows rose as she watched the thoughts play out on Elizabeth's face.

"No way. Elizabeth Marie Thornton, you didn't," she said, grabbing Elizabeth by the knee.

Elizabeth took a long drink from her beer and replied as innocently as she could, "What?" Her eyes darted away and then back to Shelly.

"You and Charlie?"

"It's not like that. We're in love with other people." *Love? Did I just say love? Hmmm.*

Shelly held up her hands and shook her head to block Elizabeth's words. "I don't want to know about it. All I'm gonna say about that, Elle, is ew; he's my brother. My little brother and no matter how grown up and handsome he is he'll always be my little brother to me."

"And did he ever grow up, mmmm-mmmm," she said with a lascivious smile and pulled on her beer. *Might as well own it, Elle.*

"Actually, Shelly, if I weren't gay I'd jump all over that myself- that man is fine!" This from Anne, a petite woman with wild curly brown hair, green eyes and fair skin who raised her beer bottle to clink with Elizabeth's glass. They laughed as Shelly made puking faces.

"*Anyway.*" She took a sip of her drink. "Mom cried when they got that care package from the bakery. That was really kind of Patty to do that."

Elizabeth waved her hand in the air to swat the mention of her mother's kindness away. She didn't want to cry again. "It was nothing, really."

"Wait a minute…that was you guys?" Bobbi asked in awe. Elizabeth just shrugged and sipped her beer.

"What am I missing here?" Hannah asked.

Bobbi indicated Elizabeth with her thumb and said, "River Rock Bakery."

Excited chatter followed that announcement and Elizabeth was a touched at the overwhelming positivity. "Very cool," Hannah said, reappraising Elizabeth.

"My brother works in your kitchen – Nate Winnig?" Jody said.

"Yea- Nate! I thought you looked familiar- You have the same eyes and hair." Elizabeth smiled remembering the wiry little man that runs the lunch kitchen. "He's done some great things for the menu over the last few years; we're lucky to have him."

Elizabeth finished her drink and rose to get another, offering to get the next round.

"Here, that's a lot to carry I'll go with you." Shelly offered. When they were away from the table, she asked, "So what do you think of Bobbi?"

"She seems really nice, and it's obvious she's in to you. If she's who makes you happy, then I'm happy for you. How were your parents when they found out?"

"They're dealing with it. The kids love her," she said with a warm smile and a look back at their table.

Elizabeth squeezed her forearm and gave her a smile. "I'm happy for you...So who would have thought we'd have run into each other here, huh?"

"I know right? So does this mean you're..."

"Gay? Well, I've never subscribed to labels. I've been with my fair share of both, so I guess you could call me fluid. My heart always chooses women, though." *The one time it chose anyone, anyway.*

It was their turn at the bar and Marty took their order, telling them that she'd send a waitress over with their drinks. Elizabeth paid her tab and was turning to walk back to their table when she felt a hand on her shoulder. She turned to see who it was and came face to face with Hailey. Her stomach was turning summersaults the butterflies were so frenzied.

"Elizabeth, hi. Fancy running into you here." She stood awkwardly, meeting Elizabeth's eyes then looking away.

"Hi Hailey. I was wondering when I would see you again." *If I would see you again...*She gave Hailey a warm smile.

"Listen, E..."

"Hey there you are – we got a table, we're up." The woman had snuck up on them both and planted a noisy kiss on Hailey's cheek. She wrapped an arm possessively around Hailey's shoulder and eyed

Elizabeth suspiciously. "Hi," she said coolly.

"Zoë DioCosta, this is Elizabeth Thornton. Elizabeth, this is my friend Zoë." She drew out 'friend' for emphasis and turned to Zoë, "Be nice."

"Ah, so you're the Elizabeth Hailey's been going on about." She traced her eyes up and down and back up Elizabeth's body in a frank appraisal that Elizabeth was pretty sure she didn't like. Zoë just smiled and said something into Hailey's ear that only she could hear, making Elizabeth feel even more uncomfortable but she refused to squirm. Hailey just shook her head and looked at Zoë with a warning in her eyes.

"Ok, I get it." She put her hands up in a gesture of surrender. "I'll just find Tracey and play this round with her," She said to Hailey. Over her shoulder she tossed a 'nice to meet you' at Elizabeth and made her way back to the pool tables.

"So…That was awkward." Elizabeth crossed her arms over her chest. "Is she why you…Are you and she…?"

"What? No. Well, not really…She's just a good friend. We're not together." She shifted under Elizabeth's gaze. "I'm not with anyone right now." She added, and then looked surprised at herself for saying it.

"Okay…Does she know that?"

"It's not like that, really. We're just friends, and sometimes…" Hailey shrugged, and looked an apology.

Elizabeth reached out and grabbed Hailey's hand and fixed her with an unwavering stare. "So why did you run the other day?"

Hailey looked like she was going to bolt, and

Elizabeth was surprised to be on the other side of this situation. Usually it was her running away just as fast as she could, always protecting her heart, never risking it even when asked to. Now that she was doing the asking, she appreciated the courage it took for any of the people in her past. She held Hailey's hand tighter and tugged on it pulling Hailey a few inches closer. "Hey, it's ok. You can talk to me."

Hailey took a deep breath and held Elizabeth's gaze for a few seconds before glancing to her lips and settling on their entwined hands. When she returned her gaze to Elizabeth's eyes her own held a pleading expression. "I've been hurt before and you scare me. Plus you're going through a lot right now and you'll be leaving eventually," she said simply, and shrugged.

Elizabeth gently ran her thumb over Hailey's knuckles. "Dance with me?"

Hailey looked out to the dance floor and back to Elizabeth like a woman drowning. Elizabeth tugged on her hand, and took a step back. "I've got you. Come on, dance with me." Hailey didn't resist.

Elizabeth led her to an empty space on the dance floor and turned to face Hailey who stepped into her embrace as they started to sway to the music. Their breath caught as they marveled at how perfectly they fit together, Hailey's pupils dilating as Elizabeth pressed their bodies closer, their breasts pressed against each other's. "I really want to kiss you again." Elizabeth told her as she ran her fingers up Hailey's neck and into her hair.

Hailey didn't say anything, but her gaze fell to Elizabeth's mouth and her lips parted; she unconsciously wet them with her tongue and Elizabeth closed the gap between them until the tiniest space remained leaving Hailey to take that last step. When she did it was tender, a gentle brushing of lips barely touching, a sharing of air. Then she pressed her lips more firmly into Elizabeth's and she groaned as Elizabeth opened her mouth, darted her tongue out deepening the kiss.

It could have been seconds or several minutes before they broke apart and leaned against the other's foreheads, their chests heaving. The song had changed from a moderate tempo to a pumping dance track, but their pace remained the same as they danced to their own rhythm.

"Oh my God," Hailey breathed.

"Can we go somewhere?"

Hailey grabbed her hand and headed toward the door, but Elizabeth tugged her in a different direction. "I need to grab my bag and jacket. Do you have anything you need to go get?"

"No, I prefer to use my pockets when I'm out- I'll come with you," Hailey said following her to the table where Elizabeth had left her things. She introduced Hailey to the group and then said her goodbyes to which they received several hoots and knowing looks and winks.

She hugged Shelly who said in a low voice, "Is that her? Oh my God, she's beautiful."

"I'll call you in a few days."

Together Hailey and Elizabeth made their way out into the parking lot stopping at the red Chevy truck. "I rode here with Zoë, so we can go together in your truck?"

"That sounds good; do you want to go to your place?"

"Yes, but first, we should probably talk about a few things. I want us to be on the same page." She kicked at some invisible rocks and ran her hands through her hair looking at Elizabeth intently.

"Ok, well we do have a 20 minute ride. We can talk on the way?" She stepped closer to Hailey. "But first..." She pulled Hailey into her arms and planted a searing kiss on her mouth and pulled away leaving Hailey breathless and disoriented. They stood there with their foreheads pressed together, panting.

"I don't know what tomorrow's going to look like, Hailey. My life is pretty fucked up right now, you know that. Jesus Christ, my mom very well might be dying and I don't know how to handle her being sick, let alone what I'll do if she dies. She's all I've got." The tears started flowing freely and her voice came out choked. She pulled back and looked into Hailey's eyes; saw that there were tears there too. "I do know that you've been the one bright spot in all this darkness for me. The one person who drives all those other thoughts out of my head for even a second, even when you're not there. You make me feel things I didn't think I was capable of feeling. You make me want things...fuck, look at me." She barked a half laugh half sob and stepped out of the embrace wiping angrily at her cheeks. "Are you sure you want any part of this? I don't even know what I can give you. I know what I want to give you. I know I don't want to hurt you..."

Hailey pulled her back into her arms and murmured soothing sounds. "Shhh, Elizabeth, it's OK. I feel the same way. I know loss. I know heartache. I know this probably won't last with everything else that's going on, but I think you're worth the risk. *We're* worth the risk." She laid soft kisses on Elizabeth's face.

"You want us to be a 'we?'" Elizabeth looked into Hailey's eyes feeling a glimmer of hope, even though she knew it was unrealistic.

"I want whatever we can be for each other for as long as it lasts."

Elizabeth laid a gentle kiss on Hailey's lips and unlocked the driver's side door. "Do you want to drive or shall I?"

~~~

Hailey drove the seven and a half miles from Luna's to her house with Elizabeth sitting immediately next to her on the bench seat, her arm around Elizabeth's shoulders holding her close. Their silence was comfortable and for the first time in her life Elizabeth felt like she belonged right where she was. She sighed and snuggled in closer feeling Hailey's warmth as the most natural thing in the world.

When they got to their destination, Hailey led Elizabeth into the house.

"I need to use the bathroom." For some reason she was feeling suddenly shy.

"It's right through there." As Elizabeth walked away Hailey ran her tongue over her teeth and grimaced to herself, "Yea me too, actually." She chuckled. "Would you like something to drink?" She asked as Elizabeth came back into the room.

"No, I'm good – do you have an extra toothbrush?"

"Yea, I do. You must have read my mind

175

actually."

"Oh my God, is it that bad?" She brought her hand over her mouth, her eyes wide.

Hailey laughed and gently pulled Elizabeth's hand down and laid a soft kiss on her lips. "I was thinking more for myself, Sweetheart. My teeth are wearing little wool sweaters."

Elizabeth blushed and grinned, "Mine too, I think." *She called me Sweetheart.*

"Well, this is something we can easily remedy. Follow me." She led Elizabeth back to the master suite and into the large bathroom and turned on a light. Elizabeth was rubbing gentle circles on her back as she opened a drawer, pulled out a brand new toothbrush and handed it to her. They brushed their teeth in silence, smiling at each other's reflection in the mirror. Nothing about performing this mundane routine with each other seemed awkward or absurd and Hailey fell in love with Elizabeth just a little bit more.

"That's better."

"Let me be the judge of that." She took Hailey in her arms and brushed their lips together in the slightest whisper of a kiss. "MMMM. Minty fresh. You'd better pee now, because I'm not going to let you out of the bed for the rest of the night." She winked at Hailey and walked into the bedroom.

Hailey's knees went weak and she had to hold herself up with the countertop. She looked at her reflection in the mirror, took in the flush of her cheeks and the goofy grin on her swollen lips. She let out a soft chuckle and shook her head at her reflection. "What are you getting into, Hails?"

When she finished in the bathroom, she turned out the light and walked into the bedroom where she found Elizabeth laying back across the turned down bed propped up on her elbows; the soft glow from the bedside lamp illuminating her features in a Honey glow.

Elizabeth sat up to meet her as she approached, her eyes darkened and hooded. She reached out both hands and slipped them under the hem of Hailey's tee shirt lifting it up to expose the flat plane of her stomach where she pressed her lips, pulling a gasp from Hailey, and laid a series of wet kisses as she lifted the shirt higher to expose Hailey's bra; the soft mounds of her breasts peaking out just over the top of the silky smooth fabric. Hailey's fingers dug into Elizabeth's shoulders as she ran her tongue over the fabric and felt Hailey's already erect nipple harden even more under the light touch.

"Oh God, what are you doing to me?"

"Not nearly everything I want to."

Soon the shirt was on the floor and Elizabeth reached around with one hand and unclasped Hailey's bra and slowly slid it down her arms and discarded it with a toss. She looked up at Hailey's face and smiled.

"You are so beautiful."

Hailey's eyes were nearly black with desire, her lips parted and her breath was shallow and fast. Elizabeth saw the pulse in her neck and knew that Hailey's heart was hammering just as hard as her own was.

"So beautiful." She took one nipple into her mouth and sucked on the tight bud, flicked it with her tongue while her hand played with the other one, which she then gave equal attention to with her tongue and teeth.

Hailey reached to pull Elizabeth's shirt off and as it left her body Hailey knelt on the edge of the bed and laid kisses on her chest as she unclasped her bra and tossed it to the floor.

Elizabeth unbuttoned Hailey's jeans and slid them and her boy-shorts off her slender hips and down her long legs as far as she could, Hailey taking over and stepping out of them easily. Elizabeth pulled Hailey in close and inhaled her scent and pressed a kiss onto the well manicured dark patch covering her mons. Unable to resist, she ducked her head slightly lower and traced her tongue along the top of Hailey's folds.

"Oh God, not yet Baby. I need to touch you too."

She lifted her hips and scooted further onto the bed as Hailey tugged her pants and panties off and dropped them to the floor. Hailey stood there a moment taking in the long frame, the smooth skin, the toned limbs, and the neatly trimmed hair of her sex glistening with arousal. She nearly swooned at the sight of it.

"You're so fucking beautiful."

"Come here." Elizabeth lay back on the bed and held out her arms in invitation. Hailey placed a knee on the mattress in the space between Elizabeth's thighs and slowly crawled up her length, sliding her own body up Elizabeth's and savoring the full contact, the press of breasts against breasts, belly against belly, hip against hip. She bent down and claimed her lips in a kiss, exploring the velvety contours of her mouth with her tongue before moving to her neck.

Elizabeth's hips lifted, searching for contact and

met a strong thigh that pressed more firmly into her, their motion matched when Hailey pressed herself against Elizabeth as they moved against each other.

Elizabeth's breath came in as a hiss. "You feel so good."

"I need you inside me."

Hailey lifted her hips when Elizabeth reached down to touch her, parted her lips and found her opening. She slid one finger in, then two and Hailey let out a moan as she pushed against her hand getting it as deep as it would go. Elizabeth slid her fingers out so slowly until just the tips remained and pushed them back in at that same exquisite pace, pulling another moan from deep within Hailey's chest.

"Oh so wet, my darling."

"That's what you do to me."

Hailey reached down her own hand and entered Elizabeth, matching pace for pace stroke for stroke. "I want you to come with me." She placed her thumb over her clit and massaged the engorged flesh with each press of her fingers. Elizabeth arched her back, the pressure of her imminent release increasing.

"Yesssss."

Hailey could feel the tendrils of her own climax starting. "Look at me, Baby. I want to watch you when you come."

Elizabeth struggled to keep her eyes open, but she somehow managed it and her thighs began to quake as Hailey's body stiffened. They came together, looking into each other's eyes and Elizabeth raised her head to kiss Hailey, their joined mouths capturing their mutual screams.

After, they lay spent and panting for long minutes, and Hailey gently pulled her fingers out making Elizabeth jerk and giggle. She lifted her hips so that Elizabeth could have her hand back and as she did so, she raised her own to her mouth and licked her fingers, a lazy smile playing at her lips. Elizabeth kissed her and tasting herself there, she was aroused all over again and rolled Hailey onto her back. She placed soft kisses down the length of her torso and as she got lower Hailey opened to her where she finally settled between her thighs and feasted.

It was nearly 4 in the morning when Elizabeth woke with a start, felt the warm body wrapped around her and for the first time in her life didn't think twice about settling back in to the embrace which instinctively tightened around her.   At some point during their evening together, something inside Elizabeth clicked into place- something she didn't even realize was askew. She couldn't suppress her smile even if she wanted to, but then her eyes widened and she shot up out of bed. *Oh my God, my mom!*

"What's the matter, Sweetheart?" Hailey's sleepy voice met her ears and she felt guilty for needing to leave this beautiful woman alone in the bed where they had just spent hours in a near perpetual state of bliss.

"I have to go to the hospital. Will you go with me?"

"Yes, of course I will."   No hesitation, no disappointment, no anger. Just a simple 'yes' as if it were a given. Elizabeth kissed her hard and she could have cried for joy at how utterly loved that simple response made her feel.

"Do you want to swing by your house and get

some fresh clothes?"

"That would be perfect- I'm sure Riley will want to go out too."

"Ok- do you want to shower here or there?"

A mischievous grin formed on her lips, "Well your shower is better equipped for two." It was another hour before they left the house.

Chapter 33

The sun had broken over the horizon and begun its steady ascent into day. The birds were chirping their morning greetings to one another as the world awoke from another night's slumber when Elizabeth and Hailey arrived at the Kathleen Roark Wing of MCMC's parking lot. They had driven over in Patty's truck, again taking advantage of the bench seat where Hailey held Elizabeth once more as she drove. Hailey joked that buckets would never do again when they could sit this close.

They walked hand in hand to the front doors of the hospital and Hailey moved to release her grip on Elizabeth, but Elizabeth stopped short and looked her in the eye.

"Regrets already?"

"No, I just don't want you to have to answer questions if you're not ready." She looked at her feet and kicked at imaginary stones on the sidewalk, not sure why she was feeling so shy and vulnerable.

Elizabeth arched a brow, "Does she know about you?"

"Yes."

"Well, she definitely knows about me, so I don't see what the problem is."

"You've told her?" Hailey's head shot up in surprise. "I thought for sure you were straight- all she ever told me about you in that way was how she didn't like Colin."

Elizabeth laughed and took Hailey's hand in her

own. "I thought last night and this morning would have proven to you how not straight I am – I guess I'll just have to keep trying. And where Colin's concerned, obviously I didn't like him all that much either. I broke it off with him over a year ago. As for what my mother knows, we hadn't discussed it until she ambushed me the other day with the mortifying knowledge that she's known since college."

Hailey raised an eyebrow in question and grinned.

"Let's just say thin walls don't keep secrets and leave it at that for now. If you want a play by play history of my sexual life, I'm not ashamed of any of it and I'll gladly give it to you, although I don't see what good it could possibly do. It has no bearing on what's happening between you and me and would probably only serve to feed whatever insecurities you might have. As for labels, well I didn't have one." She leaned in and placed a lingering kiss on Hailey's lips. When she pulled back Hailey's pupils were dilated and flashbacks of last night played in Elizabeth's mind causing her to breath to catch.

"Ok, there are a couple things in that statement that I want to come back to at some point- the 'what's happening between you and me' part and the 'didn't' part of that last bit about labels." Her grin widened.

Elizabeth just shook her head, a silly grin on her own face. "Come on, we'll get to all that."

They walked into the reception area and were greeted by June who provided them with masks and sanitizing wipes. She also grilled them about any illnesses they might be carrying and they assured her that they were healthy, showered before coming, hadn't encountered anyone else on the way and that their clothing was day-one fresh.

"It's nearly time for me to check on her now, so y'all can enter the room when I do. We'll need to be quiet because she's probably still asleep."

"How did last night go? Anything I need to know?" Elizabeth asked as Hailey squeezed her hand.

"Last night was ok. She was up sick a few times but it's nothing out of the ordinary. Her vitals seem to have leveled out but she's still running a bit of a fever. It hasn't gotten worse so that's good news."

Elizabeth's shoulders sagged with relief.

"We've got her on nutrients and liquids and meds right now and she can have water if she's thirsty. Try not to be too alarmed at her appearance. She's very ill, so she's not going to look like her usual self." June reached out to Elizabeth and gently squeezed her shoulder, giving her a gentle smile. "Try to be upbeat."

They walked down the corridor to Patty's room taking the opportunity to use the wipes June had handed them. Before they got their masks on, Hailey pulled Elizabeth in for a quick kiss and said, "It'll be alright. I'm not going anywhere."

"Thank you."

"Alright- here we go." June quietly opened the door and stepped into the room. Patty had the bed in the upright position and was flipping through one of the magazines that Elizabeth had brought over the previous day. She looked up and smiled, but it was obvious she wasn't feeling well. She looked small and frail lying in her hospital bed and there were tubes and wires and machines everywhere. The pallor of her skin made her look ghostly and drawn. It was all Elizabeth could do not to have a visceral reaction to the sight. *You just got here Elle- you can't lose it fifteen seconds into the room.*

June spoke first, her tone was cheery and Elizabeth sent up a silent thank you. "Well good morning Patty- glad to see you're awake. Look who I found lurking in the hallway." Hailey and Elizabeth stepped forward.

"Hey Patty. It's good to see you. How are you holding up?"

"Hailey. Ellie. My two favorite girls." She smiled again, this time it reached her eyes. "I'm hanging in there. How are you two this morning?" She looked at them both and frowned. "June, do they have to wear the masks?"

"They don't have to, but they should. We can take care of you, but it won't make it easier if we add to your germs."

Patty fixed June in a stare. "If this thing kills me I want to at least have been able to see my daughter's face while it happens."

"Oh Mom. Don't talk like that, you're gonna get through this." She put her hand on Patty's foot.

"Even so. You can keep your distance and I can see your face- does that sound like an alright compromise?" She arched a brow at June.

"That should be alright. Ok, all finished here Patty – I'll leave you all to visit."

"Thank you, June."

"Just press the call button if you need anything."

"Will do. Thanks."

"Now," Patty shifted her weight in the bed and adjusted the covers. "That's better." She fixed her gaze on Elizabeth's face as she removed her mask. Hailey followed suit.

"Wow. It was starting to get hot under there." She ran her fingers through her hair. "So how are you, Mom? Really. Can we do anything or get anything or…"

"I'm OK, Sweetie. Really. This chemo is kicking my ass, but I'm realizing any day that I wake up is a good day, so I'm not going to complain too loudly. I don't really want to talk about it though. So tell me what's new with you?"

Elizabeth shot a glance to Hailey and couldn't help the crimson blush spreading up her neck. Patty's eyes widened and she looked to Hailey who just returned the smile on Patty's lips.

"Well, I've been painting again. I got to thinking about what you said the other day and after looking through the stack I decided that you might be right. So I'm currently working on a couple of new canvases. I don't know how good they are, but it feels good to be back in it so I'll be happy with that."

Hailey spoke softly, "That's great, Elizabeth. I've been admiring your work for months now. I'm really glad you've decided to take it back up." Elizabeth looked up at Hailey and smiled.

The interaction between her two favorite girls was not lost on Patty. She just smiled and kept her musings to herself.

"As long as you're doing it for yourself they will be amazing, Ellie. You have so much talent. I can't wait to see the finished product." She sighed and let her head fall back into the pillows. "Before I forget, Stanley Jamison is coming over this afternoon around two to go over some legal stuff." Patty sat up and started to cough. When the coughing was finished she took a sip of the water that Hailey handed her, laid back and closed her eyes.

"We're going to let you get some rest, Patty." She put one hand on Elizabeth's shoulder and gently squeezed Patty's foot with the other. Patty only nodded.

"I love you, Mom. I'll be back later – do you want me to grab anything for you?"

"Love you too, Ellie-bean…I'm all set for now…later…happy for you…" She was already asleep. Elizabeth kissed her hand and placed it on Patty's leg and she and Hailey left the room.

They only got a few steps down the hall before Elizabeth's tears started to fall. Hailey pulled her into her arms and held her for a few minutes until Elizabeth stopped shaking and her breathing returned to normal. Hailey's own eyes were shining and she wiped them dry as they continued down the corridor and out into the day.

"Come on, let's go get some sleep."

"Will you stay with me?"

"Of course. I do have some things I need to do this afternoon, but it should only take a couple hours and I can meet you somewhere or just come over or you can come to my place or whatever works."

"That actually works out for me too; there are a couple things I should probably pay attention to as well." She pulled Hailey's hand into her lap and they drove back to Carbondale.

Chapter 34

"What the fuck?!" Elizabeth's eyes were wide and her hand flew up to her mouth as she re-read the letter from Patty's health insurance company.

'We regret to inform you…per the service level agreement…reached coverage limit…no longer able to insure you…'

She sank back against the wall of mailboxes utterly stunned. Her tears threatened to blind her, but her shock soon turned to anger and she left the post office on a mission. A few minutes later she screeched to a stop in front of the offices of Jamison and Jamison, her mother's attorneys, and jumped out of the truck.

She marched into the offices, swinging the door open and nearly barreling over some poor innocent bystander in the process. "Oh-my-gosh! I'm so sorry"

"Elizabeth!" Shelly grabbed her by the shoulders to help keep them both upright. She took in the wild eyes and red face of the out of breath woman who nearly knocked her onto her ass. "Are you alright, Ellie? What's wrong?"

"Mom's fucking insurance company is trying to deny her coverage." She was so angry that her jaw was clenching and unclenching and she was breathing like she had just run on foot from the post office. "I'm sorry Shelly, I didn't mean to nearly knock you over…I just can't believe this shit!" She roughly ran her fingers through her strawberry curls in a gesture of frustration.

"Elizabeth Thornton. What an unexpected pleasure. I'm just getting back from seeing your mother. We're all pulling for her. What brings you in to see us today?" Stanley Jamison was a small man with rodent features, his hair clipped short and silvered at the temples. Even though his was a small town law office, he was always impeccably dressed in tailored suits and shiny shoes. He'd been Patty's lawyer forever.

"Hey Stan. Can you do something about this?" She shoved the letter to him and he read it over with a grim expression. "Hmmm…I see. Well." He looked between Shelly and Elizabeth. "Recent laws have been passed to prevent this kind of thing, but a lot still depends on the wording in the contract between Patty and the insurance company. I believe we have a copy of that here on file. Why don't you give me a couple hours to look things over and I'll give you a call later this afternoon with some ideas? Do you have a number where we can reach you?"

Elizabeth reached into her bag and pulled out her card and handed it to him.

He smiled at her, "We'll get this sorted, Elizabeth. You shouldn't have to worry about this right now; you've got enough on your plate. We'll do our due diligence on this and let you know what your options are and we can move from there. In the meantime I advise you to have a conversation with the MCMC billing department and find out how willing they are to work with you while we get this straightened out."

Her breathing had calmed and her color was returning to normal, but she was still shaking. "Thank you Stanley. We really appreciate it."

Elizabeth and Shelly left the Jamison law offices together. When they were near their vehicles, Shelly reached out a hand and touched Elizabeth's arm.

"Hey. I've got some time...you wanna get a bite to eat and catch up?"

"Actually, that sounds great. I have a couple hours before I have to be anywhere and it would be good to hear what you've been up to. Where do you want to go?"

"Well, we can walk to Dos Amigos...you do still like burritos, right?"

Elizabeth nodded agreement and linked her arm with Shelly's. "So...Bobbi, huh?"

~~~

"Nope, Ms. Thornton, I've double and triple checked for you. Patty's all paid up and there's actually a sizeable credit on her account with instructions to donate the balance to MCMC once her treatment is no longer necessary, with the caveat that such a donation be made in Patty's name. Someone out there is definitely looking out for y'all."

"Is there any indication of who I might thank for this astounding generosity?" Elizabeth's perplexed expression was in direct contrast to the billing manager's benevolent and patient one.

"I'm sorry I can't give you that information, it was done anonymously. I don't even know, and even if I did I'm bound to confidentiality. That's about all I can tell you."

"Can you at least tell me when this all happened?" She put her hand to her forehead and let out a perplexed breath.

"Looks like payment was made shortly after her initial stay with us- several weeks ago. Now you know what I know." She shrugged.

"Well, thank you for your time…Janine. Have a nice day."

"You too, Ms. Thornton. Good luck."

Elizabeth couldn't deny the relief she was feeling at not having to worry about this latest twist of the screw, but she couldn't shake the nagging curiosity as to who might have done this amazingly wonderful thing.

Patty had been estranged from her own family ever since turning up unmarried and pregnant at 17. Their strict puritanical views and not wanting to tarnish their social status amongst the cream of Virginia's crop prevented them from having a relationship with their daughter and grand-daughter once the 'shame' was known. They had turned their backs on Patty and her unborn baby and left her to make her own way, cutting her off from any support when she refused to give Elizabeth up for adoption. They had hoped that their action would make Patty see the error of her ways, but all involved were stubborn as stumps and neither budged from their position once the battle lines had been drawn. There was an aunt who had kept in touch with Patty and when she died had left her the money Patty used to buy their house and start the bakery with, but there was no one else that Elizabeth could figure for it.

Elizabeth never knew who her father was; Patty refused to talk about him and referred to him only as the 'sperm donor.' So she supposed it couldn't have been anyone from his side.

If there had been a fund raiser, she would have known about it…who could it be? After much considering she decided that it must not matter since it was done anonymously. The motives must have been simple generosity and kindness rather than some strange desire to lord this over them, so she decided to let it go. She sent up a silent thank you to the cosmos and hoped that whoever it was reaped the benefit of such great karma.

Chapter 35

The next few days passed by in spurts and fits. Patty's condition didn't look to be improving and she seemed to be shrinking away, but this second round of chemo was nearly completed and then she would get a brief respite before getting more tests and embarking on whatever the next step would be.

Between visits to the hospital and visits to the bakery Elizabeth spent nearly all of her time with Hailey. She showed Hailey her old paintings and the new ones she was working on. Hailey made them dinners and they took Riley on walks and they talked about what it was like growing up and what they hoped for the future and they made love in nearly every room of Hailey's house and in a few of Patty's. When they weren't pleasuring each other sexually, they simply enjoyed the comfort of each other, spending long hours just holding each other while one or both or neither cried. Elizabeth sensed that Hailey remained somewhat guarded about certain details of her life, but she didn't press the issue owning that things would come to light in their own time given the chance.

Even though she felt it in her bones and almost slipped a few times during orgasm, she didn't yet give Hailey those 3 words that would cement their relationship. The 3 words she hadn't ever told anyone besides her mother. Hailey held back as well, but Elizabeth could see in her eyes and feel in her touch that the depth of caring was mutual. For the time being, that would have to be enough.

Chapter 36

"Hey Mom. Last day of Chemo round 2- that's pretty exciting, right?" It was a Tuesday morning and Elizabeth sat down in the chair and pulled it closer to Patty's hospital bed. It was hard to keep the concern off her face and she hoped that she was able to at least keep it out of her voice.

"Yay." The cheer Patty gave out was genuine if delivered a little flatly. "I sure as shit hope this crap is doing something good because it certainly doesn't feel like it. And I'm nearly bored out of my mind sitting in this hospital room all day!"

"Oh, Mom – do you want me to stay longer? You just get so tired I hate to keep you from resting." The guilt Elizabeth felt for all the time she was spending with Hailey twisted in her gut making her feel sick.

"No, no Darling. I didn't mean it like that. It's just…you know how much I hate being trapped like this. I get stir crazy. Even though my body still feels like hammered shit and I couldn't even if I tried, my mind wants to get the hell out of here like yesterday."

She closed her eyes and took a few deep breaths and Elizabeth draped an arm and laid her head down onto her covered legs. "I've been wanting to talk to you about something. It's important Elizabeth so I need you to pay attention."

"You know I'm undivided, Mom." She raised her head and met Patty's gaze. "What is it?"

"I don't want a funeral."

Elizabeth's eyes brimmed immediately, Patty continued. "No listen, I'm serious. I don't want to die, but I don't know if I can survive or tolerate another round of chemo if this one doesn't do the trick. I felt better when it was just cancer. At least I had some modicum of dignity. If this thing finally kicks my ass you need to know what I want. I need to know that you understand and will carry these things out." Elizabeth could only nod, her voice caught in her throat, not coming out.

"I don't want a funeral and all that expense. I'd rather whatever money would go to paying for all that unnecessary ceremonial garbage to go instead into something living, something with a future. Maybe a scholarship or a trust or whatever. Not a funeral. And I don't want people to come to some sad service and cry over my loss, I want a celebration of my life. A party where people can say a few words if they want, reminisce, maybe get drunk if they need to and then move on. Life's too short to dwell in the sad parts. I hope you'll remember that if and when the time comes. When I'm gone you have to keep going, you hear? Feel your pain and then move on. I'll never leave you Ellie, I'll always be with you no matter what." She reached her hand down and placed it on Elizabeth's hair. Elizabeth had laid her head back down and was quietly sobbing as she listened to Patty speak her last wishes. She felt little pieces of her soul getting ripped to shreds, but she had to do this, to be here for her mother.

"I want to be cremated. I think it's disgusting how they pump corpses full of formaldehyde and other embalming fluids and dress them up and paint life into their faces and then bury them into a cement lined pit. Who gives a shit what you look like when you're dead and all those chemicals and sealed coffins keep you from going back into the earth where you belong. I don't want that. I want to be spread at the top of that trail we used to hike when you were a kid. You remember the one?"

"Mushroom Rock...I remember," she whispered.

"That's right." She smiled. She laid back and took a few moments to catch her breath. Just when Elizabeth thought she drifted off to sleep, "I'm leaving everything to you, of course. Your name has always been on everything of mine anyway so that in the event of my death ownership would transfer seamlessly over to you, but I had Stanley Jamison rework my will anyway. Don't feel like you have to keep everything. I'm not going to miss it or be angry if you decide to sell or get rid of things that you don't want or need.

"If you sell the bakery, I hope you'll consider making a deal with Jake. He's a wonderful person and a fantastic manager and I know it would be in good hands with either of you."

"I'll never sell the bakery, Mom. Never."

"I'm leaving Riley to Hailey. Your life in Boston doesn't have room for a crazy dog like Riley and she loves him." Patty looked at Elizabeth and raised an eyebrow. "I daresay she loves that dog almost as much as she's growing to love you, Sweetie. You don't have to talk about it if you don't want to, but I see the way you are around each other and it makes me happy."

Elizabeth just looked up into her mother's tired smiling face. "I don't know what we can be to each other. Our lives are so different, lived out in different parts of the country. It's been intense, but it's also been so fast. I don't know what I mean to her, what I want her to mean to me…where we can go from here…"

"Do you love her?"

"I don't know." She shrugged then looked into her mother's eyes. "Yes."

"Time will sort it out then." She closed her eyes again and took several deep breaths. "There's a letter for you in the drawer there. Take it and read it whenever you're ready…I'm getting…so tired…I love you…" Patty drifted off to sleep and Elizabeth just stayed there half hugging her legs and crying quietly.

"I can't say goodbye to you, Mom. I'm not done with you. You can't die. You just can't." *God please make us strong enough to live through this.*

Chapter 37

The early morning light coming in through the space between the curtain and the window was dim and the soft sound of drizzle pattered on the window pane accompanied by the low rumble of distant thunder. Strong arms were wrapped around her middle and soft moist kisses were making their way down the line of her jaw, the breath and strawberry curls tickling her skin.

"Mmmmm. Good morning." Hailey stretched her body out, pressing it more firmly against Elizabeth's in the process, relishing in the press of flesh as she shifted onto her back to meet the travelling lips in a kiss.

"Hey." Elizabeth positioned herself so that her body was more on top of Hailey's and started kissing a path down lower.

"Oh God, what are you doing to me?"

"I should think that's pretty obvious, Lover." Elizabeth raised herself back up to Hailey's mouth to steal a quick kiss before resuming her descent. "Can I taste you?"

"I'm completely at your mercy, Elle." There was something in the way that she said it that made Elizabeth realize this was as much an admission as it was an invitation and she held Hailey's gaze with the words stuck in her throat. Instead, she lowered her lips and kissed her deeply, trying to pour everything from her heart into Hailey's mouth. When she came up for air, there were tears glistening in her eyes and she worked her way back down to lower points, burying herself in Hailey's exquisite pleasure. *If all I can do right now is show her then that's exactly what I'm going to do.*

Finally, a quivering mass of jelly barely able to form words, Hailey had to beg her to stop. She worked her way back up Hailey's body and placed tender kisses around her face, held her tight for long minutes while Hailey's breath steadied and deepened indicating sleep. Elizabeth placed one final kiss on Hailey's cheek and breathed the words she'd been aching to say her whole life: "I love you." It was true and she had no idea what to do with it.

Once she was certain Hailey was sleeping soundly, she gently pulled herself out of bed and wrote a quick note for Hailey and got dressed. She let Riley out, toweled him off when he came back in, set some food down for him and got in the truck and went for a drive. She didn't know where she was going until she ended up sitting in Charlie's driveway. After some internal debate, she decided to lightly knock on his door. If he was awake, he'd hear and answer if not it wouldn't disturb him. She was just turning to head back out into the rain when he pulled the door open.

"Elle, hi. What are you doing out here this early in the morning? It's not your mom is it?"

She answered quickly, "No. No, nothing like that."

He calmed down and rubbed his eyes as he looked at her, a big yawn escaping. His hair was disheveled and his white tee shirt was inside out looking very much like he just grabbed whatever was handy and threw it on. In a different scenario it would have been adorable.

"I didn't wake you, did I?" She gave him a sheepish grin and he stepped aside.

"Nah, I was up. Come on in out of the rain. You want some coffee?" He turned and walked to the kitchen where a pot of coffee was already brewing. He grabbed two mugs out of the cabinet and reached into a drawer for a spoon.

"I'd love some." She pulled out one of the wooden stools from beneath the breakfast bar and sat in it, looking at Charlie across the granite counter.

"So it's not your mom and you're obviously not here to make my day," he waggled his eyebrows and bit his bottom lip suggestively. "You must want to talk about Hailey. Am I right?" He handed her the carton of half and half and the sugar bowl as he spoke.

A blush rose on her cheeks and she trained her gaze to the kitchen window, watching the rain slowly slide down the glass.

"Well that explains why I haven't heard from you in a while." There was nothing in his voice but friendliness. "I take it you've come together, then."

Her blush deepened as she remembered their first time in bed and she couldn't help but smile. "You could say that. And that is why I'm here, actually. I need some advice, or a fresh perspective or I don't know. I need some help making sense of everything and you're the only person I've got here who knows the whole story and doesn't have a real stake in the outcome."

He nodded his understanding and took a long sip of his coffee. "Ok. Lay it on me."

"I love her. I love her and I don't know what to do about it. I've never been in love before- at least not like this- and as amazing and wonderful as it is, it's terrifying and it makes me feel even more vulnerable.

And I feel guilty for finding a piece of joy while my mother's in the hospital with cancer maybe dying even- and then there's the emotional hurricane about that to deal with…And I don't even live here; the life I've built is two thousand miles away…" She let her voice trail off as she realized all that she said. Her eyes widened in surprise at how it all just came spilling out.

Charlie reached out and laid a hand on top of Elizabeth's. "Does she love you?"

Elizabeth looked back to the window and shrugged. "I don't know. Well maybe that's not true…She hasn't said it, but the way she is with me," she looked back to Charlie then. "The look she gets in her eyes, the way she touches me, says my name. I have to think that she cares very deeply if it's not love."

"How does she make you feel?" He leaned back against the other counter and trained his gaze on Elizabeth, watching her body language as she toyed with the coffee mug.

"I don't know what you mean." She looked up at him with a perplexed expression.

"When you're with her, when you think about her…how do you feel?" He watched her over the rim of his cup.

"She makes me feel…safe…and like anything's possible… and valued…and just…good. No, she makes me feel great. Like my heart is going to burst with happiness. Like, colors are brighter and things taste better and I can almost believe that everything is going to be OK."

"Ok. That's good, right?" She nodded. "Alright then, your life in Boston-are you happy there? Does anything there make you feel the way Hailey does?"

"Well, I love my job. I'm good at it, it pays me really well, I know the area, and I have some friends there." She shrugged.

"You have friends in Boston who you didn't call instead of coming to talk to me about this." There was no admonishment, just a statement of fact. "It sounds to me like you feel safe in Boston and that's really its only appeal. I can understand why you don't feel like you're safe here- at least your heart doesn't seem safe, I mean. Whatever routine you had there has been disrupted and you've been thrown into chaos and you have to make whatever sense out of it you can...but Sweetie a job isn't a life and there's nothing a city so far away has that you need more than what can be found in Denver. And you have plenty of friends here who really care about you and would love to have you around for a long time." He walked over to the sink to rinse out his cup and put it in the drainer before turning back to her.

"Look. You're an insanely smart woman, Elizabeth. But, I get the feeling that you live your life too much by this," he reached out and touched her forehead, "and not enough from in here." He pressed his hand to her chest.

"I know that if you put that giant brain of yours to it you could figure out a way to make life work for you here the way you need it to. I'm not telling you that you should, just that you can and that you'll be supported. And loved." He leaned back and watched the thoughts cross her face in rapid succession. "So what are you really afraid of?"

"You'll probably think it's stupid and putting words to it makes me feel kind of silly but...I can't help but think that maybe somehow if I accept this wonderful thing happening in my life the universe is going to take something away? Does that make sense? Like, maybe you're only allowed so much joy and in order to make room for more something's gotta give and things are just too precarious with my mom and…Jesus. I don't know. I desperately don't want the other shoe to drop- you know? I almost feel like it's all too much. Like with Mom's illness and falling in love and the uncertainty of my future and everything that I hold dear. It's just so much and a big part of me wants to just disappear so I don't have to deal with any of it. It's selfish, and obviously I'm not going to run away when my mom needs me so badly, but seriously- why can't life just be easy and even?" She laughed a humorless laugh through her tears and Charlie gathered her up into his arms.

"Because the hard is what makes it worthwhile, Elle. We wouldn't be able to measure or truly appreciate our joy without pain to contrast it against- that's why life is hard. And you have to know that whatever happens with your mom has nothing to do with you and Hailey, right? You can't carry that kind of blame and it doesn't belong to you anyway." He wrapped his arm around her shoulder. "I bet if you told her these things, she'd understand and be able to help you through it. If she's half as amazing as your smile earlier told me she is, you should talk to her. But whatever you decide about your future, you have to live your life for yourself; the things you do you have to do because it's the best for you and not because you're afraid to really live."

She got up and hugged him hard, causing him to grunt and laugh. "Thanks Charlie. I don't know how you got to be so amazing, but I'm glad and you are. Now you need to follow your own advice with Diane and find your own happy ending."

"Yea- easier said than done. I talk a good game, but let's just say I know how scared you are and I'm still working my way up to it."

"You know what? I want you two to meet. Are you doing anything for dinner tonight? Say around 7:30 or so?"

"I'm pretty sure I can clear my busy schedule." He flashed a brilliant smile.

She made several phone calls on her way to the hospital that day and when she entered Patty's room, the easy smile on her mother's face and the color in her cheeks made the morning nearly perfect.

Chapter 38

'Went for a drive to clear my head. Will be at hospital by 9:30am or so. Hope to see you there today. If not call me. Or I'll call you and we can meet up later. XOXOXO Elle'

Hailey re-read the note, focused on the x's and o's and rolled over hugging Elizabeth's pillow to her face and inhaled the scent that lingered there. Hailey's heart started to race as the memory of Elizabeth's whispered words filtered back through her mind and she stretched her body out savoring the tightness and soreness she felt. It made her giggle.

She got out of bed and headed to start her morning bathroom routine when the doorbell rang. She pulled a robe off the hook and put it on, tying the belt securely around her waist as she padded barefoot through the house to the front door. There on the other side of the glass stood Zoë holding 3 to go cups and a paper bag from River Rock Bakery.

"Zoë. Come in." She relieved her friend of the tray that held the cups and gave her a one armed hug and a peck on the cheek by way of greeting. "What brings you out here this fine day?"

"Oh you know. Just on my way home from Jesse's and I thought I'd swing by since I was in the area...I saw your Jeep out front and well, you know the rest. Haven't seen you in a while." She smiled. "I stopped by your favorite bakery and grabbed a few things to eat...Is this Patty's house?" She asked stepping further into the hallway and trying to avoid getting pawed to death by the big red dopey dog.

Hailey nodded and eyeballed the bag. "I hope you have a bear claw in there," Hailey said with an impish grin. "Riley get down, that's enough. Now come on, let's go outside." She grabbed Riley's collar and led him and Zoë into the kitchen then put Riley out in his run.

"Would I let you down?" Zoë raised her sunglasses to the top of her head and seriously appraised Hailey for a long moment. "So. I see regular sex still looks as good on you as ever." She narrowed her eyes and looked into Hailey's blushing face. "I'll be damned."

"What?" Hailey took a big bite of a bear claw and reached for one of the coffees.

"Oh, nothing...I didn't see anyone else's car out front. Is Elizabeth here?" Hailey shook her head in response as she took a big bite of the bear claw. "Too bad, really. I brought an extra coffee and a few extra bites just in case. Judging from the look on your face and the fact that you're here instead of your house, I should probably make amends for my behavior at the bar that night."

Hailey just blushed and took a sip of her coffee.

"So are you going to tell me what's going on with you two or am I going to just have to make my own assumptions?"

"What is there to tell, really?" Hailey said evasively. She had only known Elizabeth for not quite a couple months, had only been involved with her for a couple weeks and they hadn't discussed their feelings for each other or what that had meant in the grand scheme of their lives.

"Well, do you really want me to break it down for you? I mean come on, let's not forget what I do for a living."

"Ok, Dr. DioCosta. You tell me." She dared, a little braver than she felt, and struck a defiant pose.

Zoë continued to watch Hailey as she spoke. "Well, I can tell by your hair and skin that you're having lots of great sex. You're trying to act nonchalant about things, but you're blushing and looking away and fidgeting- like right now," she playfully slapped at Hailey's hand as she was picking the nuts off her pastry and trying not to smile. "That tells me that you're trying to control how you're feeling or that you're not ready to admit them. Knowing you, you probably haven't told her that you're in love with her yet because you've been afraid. That's reasonable it's only been what? Two weeks?"

"Twelve days," she said sheepishly.

"Twelve days. See? That's what I mean. This is wonderful Hailey! You're in love! I've been hoping this would happen to you since I met you. I mean, granted, I was sad at first that it wasn't with me but it hasn't been anyone- don't even get me started on Gen- and now this beautiful woman shows up and look at you. You're glowing, Hailey. I haven't seen you this happy looking since before your dad passed." She put her hand over Hailey's. "Look. I know you. I know you're probably thinking about all the ways it can go wrong and all that, but look at it this way. You're ready for love now; whether you want it or not, at least your heart is ready for it, is capable of it...and whether it ends up being Elizabeth or not at least now you know you can as long as you remain open to it. That's pretty huge in and of itself." She smiled a self satisfied grin and arched a brow daring Hailey to call her wrong. Hailey just sighed and looked out the kitchen window.

"So where's the U-Haul, when's the wedding?" Zoë joked, referencing the age-old lesbian cliché.

Hailey just shook her head and looked at Zoe, the sadness had crept back into her eyes. "I don't know how any of that can happen, Zoë. Our lives are in different places."

"Bullshit."

"Excuse me?"

"I call Bullshit. BULL-SHIT. You can live anywhere in the world and do what you do. Hell, you don't have to do anything ever again for several generations and still be rich so don't give me that horsecrap about how you don't see how it can work. If you want it to work, you make it work. Simple." She shrugged and took a sip of her coffee. "Have you told her about that part of you yet?"

"I've skirted the issue because we haven't talked about how we feel about each other yet. You know how insecure I am about people just liking my money and not me. That's part of why I started fresh here. No one knows I'm *that* Jensen except for you."

"Well, just because you hated that life doesn't mean you should forget about the benefits. That's all I'm saying."

"And I appreciate tha-"

"I'm home. Hailey? Riley? Whose car is that?" At hearing Elizabeth's voice, Hailey looked at the clock on the microwave and saw that it was nearly eleven already.

"We're in the kitchen, Elle," she said as Elizabeth rounded the corner and entered the room.

Her eyes narrowed for a split second when she saw Zoë, but she recovered quickly, "Oh hi. I grabbed some sandwiches. If I had known we had company I would have grabbed an extra." She leaned over to give Hailey a quick kiss on the cheek, and Hailey wrapped an arm around her waist pulling her close and looked up into her eyes, smiling a private smile meant for Elizabeth only. Zoë looked on with an amused expression.

"Elle, you remember my friend Zoë."

"Yes Hi." She offered a hand and Zoë took it in a quick shake of greeting. "I'm not sure we were properly introduced. "I'm Elizabeth Thornton."

"Hi. Zoë DioCosta. Hailey's told me a lot about you. Hey- I wanted to apologize for the way I treated you at Luna's the other night. I was rude and it looks like I didn't need to be." She shrugged then added, "I brought you some coffee and pastries as a peace offering, but you weren't here."

The apprehension she'd been holding left her body and she relaxed more into Hailey's arm. "No, No. I get it. You didn't know me from Eve and you wanted to protect Hailey. I can put it behind us if you can." She offered a genuine smile and hugged Hailey a bit tighter then she looked around. "Where's Riley?"

"I should probably bring him in. He's been outside for a while now."

"I can go get him…you sit and visit with your friend."

"Actually I need to get going, I have a long drive

and some appointments I need to show up for." She was looking at her watch and getting up to go.

"Oh- well, thanks for stopping by. Let us know what your schedule looks like and maybe we can get together on purpose next time." Hailey gave her friend a hug.

Zoë stepped in front of Elizabeth to give her a hug and whispered in her ear, "Just take care of her, okay?" She squeezed before letting go and leaving.

As Hailey walked Zoë to the front door, Elizabeth got Riley in from outside and took the sandwiches out of the bag. She was washing her hands when Hailey came up behind her and wrapped her arms around her chest and nuzzled her neck.

"Good morning. I missed you. Did you have a nice drive? How's Patty doing this morning?"

Elizabeth closed her eyes and leaned into the embrace, temporarily lost in the hands caressing the front of her. "Mmmm. Missed you too, drive was fine, Mom's doing better..." She turned to face Hailey and kissed her soundly. She pulled back and ran a finger down the edge of Hailey's robe and pulled on it teasingly as she peeked inside.

"Please tell me you're naked under there."

"If I'm not mistaken, I owe you for this morning."

"Oh believe me. That was as much my pleasure as it was yours."

"Oh I doubt that, Baby. I'm still tingling from it." She traced her tongue along Elizabeth's ear causing her to shiver. "Come on, come to bed with me."

Elizabeth reached down to the belt holding

211

Hailey's robe closed and with deft fingers pulled it loose to allow the robe to fall open. "I'll go anywhere with you, Darling, but first I'm going to have lunch in my mother's eat in kitchen." And she did.

~~~

It was half past 2 in the afternoon when they were getting out of the shower. Elizabeth's cell phone was ringing and she ran to answer it thinking it might have been the hospital. She flipped though the call log and saw that it was Harry Gordon. She apologized to Hailey and stepped into the back room, she redialed the number.

"Hi Harry, it's Elizabeth. I'm sorry I missed your call…"

Hailey walked from the bathroom to the bedroom, rubbed her hair with a towel and began pulling some clothes out of the overnight bag she had packed for herself a few days before. Once dressed, she gathered up hers and Elizabeth's worn garments and headed to the laundry room to start a load to washing.

She went back into the bathroom and gently ran a comb through her hair to get rid of any lingering tangles, then pulled it into a loose knot that rested at the nape of her neck. When she was finished with her hair, she walked back into Elizabeth's room and caught her as she was lowering a shirt over her head. Seizing the opportunity, she bent her head to playfully place a raspberry on Elizabeth's stomach, but instead, she startled Elizabeth and before she knew it Hailey was stunned and on the ground a sharp pain radiating from her cheek where she caught a surprised elbow.

"Oh my God! Sweetie are you alright? I'm so sorry!" Elizabeth knelt down onto the floor in front of

Hailey, gently reaching to pull Hailey's hand away from her face. "Let me see it, Love." She murmured softly.

Hailey's heart skipped a beat at the endearment and she let Elizabeth take her hand and look at her cheek. She sucked in her breath when Elizabeth gently raked her fingers across it and Elizabeth grimaced in apology.

"I don't think you'll have a black eye but we should probably ice it anyway. I'm so sorry." She gently laid a soft kiss on the wounded cheek.

"It's alright. It was kind of silly sneaking up on you like that," she said, chagrined.

"No, it wasn't silly, it was sweet and I am really very sorry I clocked you. Come on, I think there's a bag of peas in the freezer with your name on it. Later if it still hurts and you haven't headed for the hills, perhaps I can kiss it and make it feel better."

Once Hailey's face was as cold as the peas, they went to   visit   Patty.

Chapter 39

Charlie greeted Hailey and Elizabeth in the parking lot of Kelly's Chop Shop, a new gastro-pub in Glenwood Springs. Once the hugs and introductions were passed around they made their way inside. "I haven't been here yet, but I hear the steaks and burgers are really good. The girls already grabbed a table and there's someone I'd like you to meet; I hope you like her as much as I do."

Elizabeth grabbed his arm and looked at him questioningly and he grinned widely, "I decided to take my own advice."

"Good for you, Charlie!" She playfully chucked him on the shoulder.

The inside of Kelly's looked like a large gutted auto mechanic's garage decorated with an ultra-industrial style, all brushed steel and clean lines. The lighting was muted and facilitated by hand blown glass bulbs in various colors hanging down over the tables. Soft music from bands like The Ting Tings and the XX filtered in from strategically placed speakers and helped set a fun and friendly mood. The bustling kitchen was open concept, located along the back of the space; the sounds and smells of various dishes being prepared filled the room.

Shelly and Bobbi were in an animated conversation with a third woman at the wrap-around booth they had gotten for the group. As they approached, laughter erupted and the stranger brushed a lock of her chestnut hair off her face, tucking it behind an ear. Shelly and Bobbi looked up and greeted them with smiles, but the brunette sitting with them only had eyes for Charlie. It warmed Elizabeth's heart when she looked sideways at him and saw the sparkle and smile in his eyes.

"Elizabeth, Hailey- I believe you already know my sister Shelly and her partner Bobbi." Shelley and Bobbi both greeted them warmly, shaking hands and scooting their bags over to make room. The woman reached out to Charlie who took her hand as he was sitting down. "And this beautiful creature is Diane," he said with a smile and kissed her hand. She reached out and shook Elizabeth and Hailey's hands in greeting.

"It's so nice to finally meet you. Shelly has been regaling me with stories from when you were kids together. It's nice to finally put a face to them." Hailey took Elizabeth's jacket and with her own hung them on the nearby coat hook before sitting.

"It's nice to finally meet you too. Charlie told me you're from Texas originally?" And the conversation was started. They quieted only when the server stopped by their table to get their orders, sharing facts about themselves and stories of each other and the times they'd spent together. When the food came it was delicious, the couples exchanging food with each other, friends and siblings stealing fries or other small morsels off each other's plates and before they knew it the evening was over, much later than they realized. In the parking lot, they continued to talk and made plans to get together again soon. All in all it was a good night.

Hailey and Elizabeth walked back to Hailey's Jeep hand in hand. "I had a really nice time tonight, Elizabeth. Your friends are warm and welcoming; I can see why you like them."

Elizabeth smiled, "I had a nice time too. I wouldn't mind doing that again. But now," She stretched and yawned, leaned into Hailey to lay a lingering kiss on her lips. "I just want to be alone with you."

"Mmmm. That can be arranged."

Chapter 40

"Well, I'm not going to beat around the bush." Dr. Martin's face was neutral, but there was a glint in his eyes that hadn't been there the last time they were waiting to hear results. Elizabeth tried not to be too hopeful, but the electricity of their anticipation was palpable and charged every corner of Patty's small hospital room. She held Patty's hand in her own and gently squeezed reassurance as Patty sat trembling. It had been the better part of a month since Patty was first hospitalized, the second round of chemo had been completed and nearly 3 weeks of post-chemo recuperation had all led to this moment.

"Preliminary tests show a complete eradication of the cancer cells." He smiled at them for the first time with a real, warm smile that reached his eyes. Patty let out a gust of air and her body sagged with the relief, tears of relief already streaming down her cheeks. Elizabeth let out a 'whoop!' and turned to her mother giving her a tight hug.

"We're not out of the woods yet," Dr. Martin cautioned and cleared his throat, looking into the expectant eyes of the women sitting before him. "Your body seems to be in remission, but your blood cells are still struggling to rebuild- particularly your white cells and platelets. This means that you are still at a very high risk for secondary infections, and there's still a chance the cancer could come back." He placed his elbows on his knees and steepled his hands in thought as he leaned forward in the chair.

"There are a few options for post remission treatment and stem-cell transplant seems to be the most effective, but it's not without risk. There's a condition called graph vs. host disease or GVHD in which the transplanted cells attack the host body which can lead to a whole slew of other problems and in rare cases even death- although, we're usually able to combat it fairly well. When it is successful, it helps the body to rebuild itself more quickly and also goes after any lingering cancer cells that might remain or develop. Then over the course of the following months, regular maintenance chemo is recommended to help ensure the cancer doesn't come back. While it remains unpleasant, it's nothing as severe as what you've been going through. The treatment we've had you on was very aggressive.

"If you decide to go this route, we'll get the procedure scheduled and move forward. I've brought in some information about it as well as some regarding other possible treatments that you could undergo instead. Whichever treatment you choose, please keep in mind that post remission treatment is a necessary part of beating cancer in the long term. Too many patients quit coming in once they hit remission thinking they've got it licked only to come back a few months or even a year or so later as sick as or sicker than before with a worse prognosis."

He reached out and gripped Elizabeth's and Patty's hands and then stood up. "I'll let you two discuss this amongst yourselves. We have some time before you decide. Whichever treatment you go with, I want to give your body a few more weeks to get stronger first."

Patty asked, "When can I go home?"

He looked between them for a moment as if

deciding his response. "Well, like I said, you're still very susceptible to infection so you'll want to avoid public places and sick people. Any visitors you have will have to be thoroughly disinfected prior to seeing you…but, I think it's safe to say that you can go home in a couple days. I'll want to see you at least once a week to run some tests and monitor your progress, though. I'll start the paperwork." He offered another smile and left the room.

Is it too soon to hope? Elizabeth squeezed Patty's hand and smiled at her through the tears still pooling in her eyes.

Chapter 41

"That was a lovely speech Hailey." Peter Manning stood next to Hailey in the California sun with an arm around her shoulders and gave her a light squeeze as she wiped a stray tear from her cheek. "And this sculpture is perhaps the best one you've ever made. He would have been proud."

Hailey looked sideways at Peter and laughed although there was little humor to it. "You know he thought my art was a frivolous waste of time, Peter."

"No, I think he just wanted to make sure you had something to fall back on, to ensure your independence and potential for success. I know you think he wanted you to replace Fitch and follow in his footsteps where Fitch couldn't, and maybe that was partially true." He looked into her face and noted the incredulous expression there. It only took him a second to decide. "There's something you need to see." He grabbed her hand and led her away from the crowd of people, out of the park and to his waiting Range Rover.

She offered no protest, as whatever this mystery was had to be better than forcing smiles and polite conversation with the social elite of Atherton, at an event that only opened wounds both fresh and old. Then she thought of Elizabeth and longed for her embrace, the comfort of her smile, of her arms, of her mouth. *Would dad have approved of her? Of us? US. I like the sound of that.* She rolled the thought around in her mind a little while longer as the California landscape passed by unnoticed.

"Where are we going?" She asked, realizing they

had left the city.

"You'll see. Apparently, I should have done this a long time ago, and frankly I thought you must have already known given that it's your property now."

She had inherited a rather large estate when her father died, but she didn't have the time or will to sift through every single item of it. There was simply too much; too much pain, too many memories, too many reminders of the father she had lost.

The Range Rover traversed its way onto a winding mountain road that ascended the foothills of Paz Peak. They turned off the paved way onto a rutted dirt drive. A few minutes later the trees opened up in front of them to reveal a modestly sized log cabin style home, similar in outward appearance to Hailey's house in Colorado- all wood and stone and windows. Her breath caught in her throat.

"I remember this place…we used to come here before…" Her voice trailed off and she struggled to catch her breath.

Peter shut off the engine and they sat there for a few moments looking at the house through the windshield. "Phillip brought me here once right after I graduated college. You and he weren't talking at the time, one of the many standoffs between the two of you regarding the direction of your future. I approached him about it when I was home one weekend. I asked him why he was so hard on you all the time, why he was so adamant that you give up your dreams. He brought me here." He opened his car door and moved to step out. "Come on, you need to see this."

He stepped around to the front of the vehicle and reached out his hand to Hailey as she walked up to him. She took it and they walked hand in hand up to the thick oak door. Peter reached up to the small ledge created by the head jamb and found the spare key handing it to Hailey. She looked at him with a mix of fear and sadness and curiosity in her eyes then took the key and slipped it into the lock.

The door swung open with a creak and they stepped into the dim room. Peter ran a hand along the wall in search of the light switch. When he found it, the light came on revealing a large great room. Hailey was surprised at the lack of dust.

"My parents have been coming out here once a month to clean and check on things." He ran a finger across the mantle. "They must have been here recently, too."

Hailey just stood in the entry way, her mouth agape. On display throughout the space were pictures of her and her mother and brother and father all in various shots both posed and candid. There were even pictures of the Manning's and others of distant relatives and friends that Hailey didn't remember. On one shelf there were several trophies and framed certificates and as she stepped near to get a closer look, she realized it represented Fitch and all his accomplishments and promise. All reminders of what once was, a happier time.

Intermingled throughout the furniture of warm mahogany and chocolate leather were pieces of her artwork; drawings she'd made, paintings that Phillip had had framed, sculptures, her attempts at pottery... all things she thought had been lost for years, even things she had forgotten making, from the time she was a young girl right up through college. She realized that some of the things her father had had to have been purchased at one or more of the many art shows that she had been included in, which struck her deeply since she had no idea he'd even been aware or interested. As she took it all in a shuddering breath escaped her and she felt the moisture on her cheeks from the tears streaming freely.

"This is where he came to think. Surrounded by the things that reminded him most of the people he loved dearly." Peter stepped to one of the larger sculptures in the room and ran a finger along its surface, then slowly paced around the room. "He told me that he was so hard on you because the world is a hard place, filled with hard victories and harder lessons. He wanted you to be able to stand on your own two feet despite the fact that you didn't have to. That he'd never been more proud of you than the day you stood up for your dreams and went to RISD-even against his protests, even prouder when you graduated. He knew you conceded to Brown to make him happy and that happiness came from knowing that even if for whatever reason your dream had to become a hobby that you'd be able to make it in the world- that if all the money suddenly disappeared, you'd be able to find your own way." Hailey looked into Peter's face, his own cheeks wet with tears and sympathy in his eyes. "He also knew it was selfish to push the business on you, but you were so smart and so eager to please him and he was so reluctant to let you go. You were the last real family he had, Hails. He knew you'd eventually choose your own path, that you'd do your own thing and make your own life, but for the little bit he had you with him in his world he allowed the fantasy some indulgence. And, he reasoned that since he wouldn't always be around to run it, someone had to know how to do it the way he wanted it, so they could make sure the next person held up to it. He told me that he was hedging his bets with me, by nudging me in the same direction." He laughed then.

"Why didn't he tell me any of this?" She wiped at her wet cheeks once again.

Peter just shrugged. "I don't know. Maybe he didn't get the chance. Maybe he thought you'd be a stronger person if you didn't know. Maybe he thought you'd be mad at him or that you'd stop fighting for it if you knew all along that you could have it. I can't answer that for you." He put his hands in his pockets and rocked up on the balls of his feet. "Anyway, I'm going to go have a look around the grounds. You should check out the other rooms while you're here. I think there's probably more here that you need to see."

She looked at him for a long moment and whispered 'thank you' to his retreating figure.

Chapter 42

"Mom, I'm home," Elizabeth called from the front door. Patty had been back home for almost 2 weeks and she seemed to be getting better and stronger every day. It was the nearly August and all the trees had their leaves, Patty's peaches were the size of racquet balls, the flowers were in the full swing of their summertime show and the birds that had flown off for the winter had come back and started the next generation. The whole world felt alive and full of possibility.

Elizabeth carried the groceries into the kitchen, set the bags on the bar and moved further into the house, "Mom? Where are you? Riley?" She called.

She moved down the hallway and found Patty's bedroom door open, her bed empty and made. She then went into the other rooms and found them empty as well. A sinking feeling formed in the pit of her stomach and she swallowed the rising panic. "Hello?" She called again.

She heard a scratching sound coming from the sun room and went in to see what was up. Riley was pawing at the back door trying to get to Elizabeth. When she approached the door to open it for him, he ran over to one of the lounge chairs on the patio and nuzzled his head under Patty's still hand and let out a high pitched whine.

"Mom?" Terror iced Elizabeth's blood as she approached the chair where her mother lay still. "Mom!" Hot tears spilled from her eyes and her chest constricted making it hard to breathe as she walked around so that she could see her mother's face and reached out a hand to touch her skin. It was warm from the sun, but her hand was not the soft and supple hand she knew. Instead, it had a strange stiffness and lifelessness to it and Elizabeth knew immediately that her worst fears were true. She had only been away a few hours, having gone into town to run a few errands and pick up stuff to make dinner. Hailey was due to return from her trip to California shortly and they were all planning to spend their traditional Wednesday night together.

Elizabeth looked into the peaceful face of her mother and thought to herself *it looks like she's sleeping*. Elizabeth knew differently from the non-responsiveness and the lack of breathing and pulse when she checked, the hollow cheeks and set of her jaw but if only for a second she wished she could fool herself into thinking this was all just a misunderstanding. That Patty would wake up and everything would be ok.

Instead she fell to her knees and let out a series of wails, rested her head on Patty's legs and cried. Hollow and desolate didn't begin to describe the pain shredding her guts as she folded in upon herself trying to insulate from the truth of the situation.

Sometime later- it could have been 10 minutes or several hours- Elizabeth had lost all track of time, she felt a hand on her back and she nearly registered the feel of a soft warm body wrapping itself around her with strong arms and legs as if to protect her from the horror of this day. She heard as if from a great distance the sound of crying and of someone calling her name, the volume increasing as her awareness began to surface, and vaguely she thought that the sound was soothing and somehow familiar. She raised her head to look with eyes that did not see, not really. She laid her head back down onto her mother's leg and closed her eyes once again.

Chapter 43

"Yes, thank you. We'll be right here. Just come right on in, the door will be unlocked." Hailey hung up the phone and wrung her hands, pacing the kitchen floor a few times before getting a bottle of water out of the fridge and going to Elizabeth who sat on the couch in the sunroom. The police and someone from the coroner's office would be there shortly to take Patty and their statements as is standard procedure when someone dies.

Elizabeth was half sitting, half lying on the couch, her cheek resting on the arm as she stared blankly out the window in the direction of where Patty laid. Hailey approached her softly, remembering how she herself had felt when Nonna and her father each passed away, that same hot knife of emptiness threatening to slice her open again as the truth of Patty's death sank in.

"Elizabeth, Sweetheart, can you drink some of this for me?" She was kneeling in front of Elizabeth, a hand on her knee, love and concern both evident in her eyes. Her heart broke for this beautiful woman before her.

A tear spilled over Elizabeth's eye and ran a slow path down the side of her nose. With a fingertip, Hailey caught the tear and brought it to her own lips, tasting the salt of Elizabeth's agony and thinking to herself that she would swallow it all if she could. Elizabeth looked at her then, her features on the brink of crumbling beneath the weight of her pain. She whispered, "She's really gone, isn't she."

"Yes, Baby. I'm so sorry." Hailey wrapped Elizabeth in a warm hug and pressed kisses into her cheeks and onto her eyes and into her neck and they held each other as the tears and sobs loosed themselves once more.

Moments later, Hailey heard the front door open and someone called from the entry way. "Hello? I'm Officer Reyes. You reported a death?" She called tentatively from the foyer as she stepped further inside. Hailey gave Elizabeth one more squeeze then released their embrace as she sat back and wiped the tears from her face with both hands. As she approached the young officer she reached out a hand in greeting.

"Yes, Hi. I'm Hailey Jensen, a friend of the family. I called to report the death of Patty Thornton."

~~~

After what felt like several hours of going over the events and watching the coroner do his preliminary examination, taking liver temp and writing out the details for the death certificate, finally they had wheeled Patty's body out to the waiting ambulance where Hailey was ensured that a full autopsy would be done as is the case with deaths like this; regardless the lack of foul play, unless the cause of death is readily known an autopsy is performed to make that determination.

Hailey went back into the house and washed her hands in the kitchen sink, filled a glass of water and guzzled it all down. Her shoulders slumped and she hung her head, closing her eyes to clear her mind while stifling the urge to vomit.

She wandered through the house looking for Elizabeth, having noticed that she left the sun room couch when they went out to see to Patty's remains.

She found her buried beneath the covers of her bed, curled up in the fetal position, her knees up to her chest. Hailey kicked off her shoes and pulled off her pants and gingerly climbed into the bed behind Elizabeth and wrapped her body around her lover once more, hoping to be a protective shell for her. As Elizabeth's body instinctively snuggled into the warm embrace, Hailey decided not to worry about anything just then; the business of death could wait a few more hours while the living got some much needed rest.

Chapter 44

Hailey was still wrapped around her when Elizabeth opened her eyes several hours later. A quick glance at the alarm clock's angry red digits let her know it was almost one in the morning. She gently pulled herself free from Hailey's embrace, immediately missing the warmth, but needing to go to the bathroom and already restless.

Her mind was numb and racing at the same time, numb by the pain of yesterday and racing to everything that needed to be done, all the arrangements and phone calls that needed to be made. As she sat on the toilet staring at the wall she remembered the conversation and envelope that Patty had given her that day in the hospital. Was it really only a few weeks ago?

She pulled up her pants and splashed some water into her face then headed into the den where she had been keeping her brief case and computer tote and booted up the iPad, opening the email app and sending off a note to Harry Gordon regarding the death of her mother and her need for additional time off to process everything. She then jotted down a quick list of the things she'd need to get done within the next few days, hoping that nothing got forgotten. Once that was done, she opened the search tool and found the numbers for the local funeral home, her mother's favorite florist, and several appropriate locations for the 'celebration' that her mother had requested in lieu of a funeral. She had briefly considered closing the bakery down for a day and having it there, but there was too much going on to shut it down for a whole day, so she chose instead to find an afternoon opening at one of her mother's other favorite local spots, compiling a list of numbers to call at some point after the sun rose. She then went through the desk drawers until she found Patty's address book and placed it with the lists of people and places to call in the morning. It took about an hour to complete and when she was done she still felt empty despite her accomplishment.

She took the envelope her mother had given her and went into the kitchen to grab a drink of water, finally registering thirst. She sat at the breakfast bar and fingered the edges of the envelope, both curious and afraid of what it might contain. Curious because she had so many questions, so many things they'd never discussed and afraid because she knew how much it would hurt to know this would be the last time her mother would ever address her in any way. If she held on to it, its message could be held on to as well and it would be like holding onto her mother. But she knew that she needed to read it, knew that Patty wanted her to know whatever she had to say. She ran her finger under the edge of the flap and eased it open, careful not to tear the paper.

My Dearest Elizabeth, my daughter, light of my life:

As I lay here in the hospital writing this I am reminded of the baby journal I kept when I was pregnant with you and the first note that I ever wrote to you. I remember wondering what you would look like, what you would sound like. Would I love you as much as I should? Would you love me? Would I mess you up somehow? Was I capable of being a good enough mother to raise you right? Could I give you everything you need?

Up until a few weeks ago, I didn't think I could get more scared. I was so afraid that I wouldn't be able to do it and so determined that you would be mine. And I was all alone; it was just me and you. Somehow we did it, though, didn't we?

I have loved you every single day of your life since before you were born and you have been the best daughter a mother could have ever hoped for. You have made me so proud. Not just in the things that you've accomplished in your professional life, but in the woman I see in you when you let your guard down. You've always been so guarded, so reserved, holding your cards tight to your chest. I know you were taking it all in and learning from everything around you, but Sweetheart, I hope you'll heed my advice when I tell you that you need to get out there and live life. Don't be afraid of the things I was afraid of because in looking back I realize there wasn't anything to fear. Pain is how you measure joy and that's not something to fear. Don't get me wrong, I've had a lot of joy in my life but I could have used a little more pain. That would have meant that I was taking risks and experiencing the full spectrum of what life has to offer. Don't hide yourself away in work like I did.

The only regret that I have in raising you is that I didn't set a better example in how to love. Or better yet, in how to let yourself be loved by someone; how to not be afraid of love.

I hope you'll allow yourself the freedom to express your love once you've accepted that she's the one. You know who I'm taking about and let me just say that when I see how you respond to her my heart swells with joy because I know you've found something in Hailey that few people ever really find in another human being. Love. It's a gift Sweetheart. It's a risky proposition, but it's also a gift. Don't do what I did and let fear of getting burned keep you from dancing around the flames.

Which leads me to the next part of this letter to you. I know you've always had questions growing up and I've always been closed off about how you came to be and why you don't have a dad and everything related to that whole situation. I know that all of it made life harder on you than it needed to, and for that I'm sorry. The plain and simple truth is that your father was a boy I fell in love with, who I thought loved me back and who I had planned to run away with. We were together only the once, the night he declared his intentions to me, and soon after I learned I was pregnant. He said he would marry me, that we could be together, to make a family and have a life, but his father wouldn't hear of it. Their family was too far above ours to allow such a thing. A Senator's son and a farmer's daughter- the nerve! They even went so far as to offer to pay for an abortion- something unheard of in Virginia in those days, but there was no way I was going to destroy the most beautiful thing in the world.

I was crushed when William dumped me; he was my first and I loved him. I thought he loved me. I never knew if it was because he was a weak and spineless little shell of a man or if it was because he never really loved me and never intended to marry me in the first place. Just got what he wanted and tossed me aside…Either way I soon realized I was better off without him. You should never get tied to someone who isn't willing to put up a fight to keep you.

When I met him, William Gray was just a boy in college pretending to be a man. Anyway. That's all in the past, and now you know who your father is. I didn't want to tell you when you were younger because it was embarrassing, and painful, and he really and truly amounted to nothing more than a sperm donor anyway. But I think you're old and smart enough now to be able to handle it.

I have a sister, your aunt. Her name is Denise Walters. She's a couple years younger than me. If this cancer kills me, I would appreciate it if you would let her know. I know my relationship with my family hasn't been all I dreamt it would be when I was a little girl, but they deserve to know about me and about you and about everything you're willing to tell them. It's funny how in what feels like the last moments things you think are so important when you're full of life don't really matter in the end, and things you thought were put away for good seem to pop back into the fore. Anyway, her contact info is in my address book...

I'm not afraid to die. I've lived a good life, raised a beautiful and wonderful girl into an amazing woman, worked hard to make something for the community and even had some fun along the way. I've made my peace with my God and although I have no desire to meet my maker any time soon, I'm ok with it if it's my time.

I do worry for you though, Ellie-bean. I suppose it's a mother's lifelong burden to worry over her children and I do so worry over you. It's all up to you now, and I know that whatever you decide in life it'll be what's right for you and I'll be proud. Just follow your heart, use your head and remember everything I taught you. Just know that I'll never leave you. I'll be there with you through it all. I'm not going away, just changing shape is all.

One last thing: This might come as a surprise to you, but your father wasn't the last man I loved. There were a few who stirred my soul and shook me up over the years, but the one that endures in my heart has always been Ben Thompson. He doesn't know it because I never told him, and we haven't seen each other in a long time. I know that he found a woman who could give all of herself to him in a way I couldn't or wouldn't when he married Janie and I have made my peace with that. But oh! That's the one thing I would do over if I could. I'd take my own advice, grab life by the horns and rock his world but good- the way he rocked mine. And I'd stay instead of running away. I'd say yes if I had the chance all over again. Yes yes yes!

So that's it. I love you. I'm not leaving you. I'll always be alive in your heart. And most importantly: LIVE LIFE! They say youth is wasted on the young…well. I don't know about that, but I know that we take too much for granted and I'm changing it to 'health is wasted on the healthy.' Live life. Love. Have fun. In the end all we have are our memories, so make them count.

Patty, your adoring mother

Chapter 45

Hailey awoke to an empty bed. She reached out an arm to feel the sheets and they were cold, the clock on the nightstand told her it was just after 3 in the morning. Rising from beneath the warm covers she rubbed her eyes and stifled a yawn and padded down the hall to the bathroom. As she entered the main living area of the house, she noted a light on in the kitchen and went to it in search of Elizabeth.

Elizabeth was sitting at the breakfast counter, her head resting on her arms, her face slack with sleep. Hailey reached out a tentative hand and touched her shoulder, spoke softly to her.

"Elle?"

Elizabeth murmured incoherently and shifted her head slightly but remained asleep. Hailey rubbed her back a little harder and spoke into her ear, pressing a kiss into her cheek, "Sweetheart."

"Hmmmm?" Elizabeth stirred then and her eyes fluttered open.

"Come on, Sweetheart. This stuff can wait 'til tomorrow. Come on." Hailey extended a hand and Elizabeth took it, using it to help herself up. She looked at Hailey and the expression in her eyes broke Hailey's heart. She wiped the sleep from her face and let herself be led through the house. Riley followed close behind.

When they got to the hallway, Hailey made a decision and instead of taking her to the bedroom, she took her to the bathroom. Elizabeth just stood there looking utterly defeated and Hailey moved quickly to run the shower and started gently removing Elizabeth's clothes. Elizabeth started to protest, but Hailey hushed her.

"Let me take care of you. Please." Elizabeth allowed her to remove her shirt and stepped out of her pants and underwear when Hailey pushed them down. Then Hailey removed her own clothes and stepped into the shower, pulling Elizabeth in behind her.

They stood under the water as it cascaded down their bodies; Hailey pushed Elizabeth's hair out of her face then put some shampoo in her hands and washed it, massaging her scalp and neck in the process. Elizabeth let out a groan and relaxed into the touch. Then Hailey did the same with conditioner and rinsed that out as well pouring all her love into her fingertips as she did. Then she put some body wash into the pouf and gently covered Elizabeth's body with deliciously scented suds, then used her hands to make sure there wasn't a spot missed as the water rinsed the rich lather away. If she noticed Elizabeth's tears, she didn't say anything about them; she simply accepted them and continued on her gentle mission to pour love into her in this intimate way.

Hailey turned the water off and gently squeezed the excess from Elizabeth's hair then her own and reached for one of the large fluffy towels that hung just outside door. She wrapped her own body first then took the other and gently rubbed the water from Elizabeth's hair and skin, then pulled the robe from the hook and draped it over Elizabeth's shoulders. She took her hand and led her into the bedroom.

Elizabeth sat on the bed watching Hailey as she rubbed the water from her hair and skin. Hailey reached for the lotion on the bureau and squeezed some into her hand gesturing for Elizabeth to lie back.

"You don't have to do this," Elizabeth said, her eyes locked with Hailey's and an expression of wonder on her face. *No one has cared about me like this in a very long time- maybe ever.*

"I want to. Let me take care of you." She rubbed her hands together and began massaging the cream into first Elizabeth's right leg, then the left. She squeezed more lotion into her hands and began rubbing it into Elizabeth's abdomen, up to her breasts and shoulders, her arms and her hands.

"Let me do the back of you." She murmured and Elizabeth rolled over onto her stomach. Hailey rubbed the lotion into her back and ass and the backs of her legs, taking her time and commenting on the various knots of stress that Elizabeth held in her shoulders and neck.

When Hailey was finished, Elizabeth's body was completely relaxed and she laid a soft kiss on her shoulder then quickly moisturized herself. When she looked back to the bed Elizabeth was laying on her side, her head propped on her hand.

"Come here," she said and extended her free hand to Hailey and pulled her into a lingering kiss. She rolled on top of Hailey's body, feeling her skin and began laying kisses and nibbles along her collar bone. Hailey let out a gasp, her body reacting to the heat of the kisses and the tickle of Elizabeth's breath.

'Live life.' Her mother's words rang through her mind. *I want to love you. I need to feel something other than this pain…you make me* feel. *Please let me feel this.*

She kissed her again, this time deep and probing

as Hailey surrendered beneath her. What started off as gentle soon became a frenzied crush of lips and teeth as the heat ratcheted between them and the kisses became a nearly bruising dance. They pawed and clawed at each other, both fighting for dominance, each gripping the other as though the world were about to burst into flames taking them with it, as if letting go would cause the other to disappear. Elizabeth pulled back and looked into Hailey's hooded eyes, nearly black with desire and something more, something raw and vital. Her skin was flushed, her lips swollen and nearly crimson, her chest heaving to catch her breath. *So very much alive.* Elizabeth realized that Hailey needed this just as badly as she did. She pinned Hailey to the bed with hips and limbs and ran her hand down her abdomen to the heat between her legs and entered her, kissing her again deeply as she did so. Hailey consumed her, took her inside of herself and held her there, silky warm flesh hugging fingers, mouth sucking tongue as each pumped into her again and again. This was life. The source of everything, primitive and natural and Elizabeth couldn't get enough. When Hailey came, it was hard and fast and Elizabeth continued to stroke every last delicious drop of pleasure out of her, wringing it from her as she rode the waves but instead of stopping, she added another finger and slipped down to place her mouth over Hailey's engorged flesh, tasting the salty sweet tanginess of her. Her hand slowed as she licked up one side and down the other, Hailey's hips rising and shifting trying to get the contact she most needed. Hailey gripped the sheets, nearly pulling them off the bed and when Elizabeth finally took her into her mouth Hailey cried out, a guttural moan from deep within her chest as she came a second time. This time the sound that started out as a voicing of pleasure became a crushing sob of grief and as Elizabeth slowly removed her fingers Hailey's shoulders shook not only from the joy of her overly sensitized sex, but also from sorrow.

Elizabeth moved back up the length of Hailey's body and held her close. "Shhh, I've got you." She murmured as her heart broke all over again, this time for Hailey's pain instead of her own. "I'm right here." Hailey buried her face in Elizabeth's neck and sobbed. She let it all out, all the sorrow and grief she'd been holding onto, for her mother, for her father, for Nonna and Patty, for Elizabeth. A distant part of her felt guilty for giving into it when Elizabeth needed her but she couldn't help it. Something inside of her had shifted and her soul purged itself of its own accord.

Some long moments later, Hailey pulled back and looked into Elizabeth's eyes, lifted her hands to cup her face and kissed away the tears there. When she should have been exhausted, she found herself energized and ready to give as much of that vitality back to Elizabeth. Over the course of the next few hours, they took turns giving and taking, fucking and crying and loving with each other until well after sun up. Finally sated and spent they lay in each others arms sweaty and limp. They might have lain like that for the rest of eternity if not for Riley scratching at the door telling them to get up and let him out.

Chapter 46

"I don't know, Peter. I mean, it's not like we professed our love to each other. We hadn't talked about the future or where things were going between us." Hailey sat slumped on her couch, the salty streaks of dried tears on her cheeks, her eyes swollen and red. It had been just over 2 months since Patty's funeral. In that time Elizabeth had become distant, nearly despondent as the grief over Patty's death started to hit her and sink in. She had pushed Hailey away, had pushed everyone away, locking herself in Patty's house and seemingly folding in on herself. Just over six weeks ago, Hailey startled awake to Riley who had jumped up on her bed and proceeded to lick her face. She had been excited when she thought that Elizabeth was with him, but that soon eroded to bitter disappointment when she found the note on her kitchen counter.

Hailey,

Gone back to Boston. Need to sort through some things. Please take care of Riley.

Elizabeth.

"And you haven't heard from her since you found the note?" Peter Manning handed Hailey a cocktail, which she took gratefully and drank nearly half of before responding.

"No. You know what I know. She just up and went back to Boston without another word. I've left her many messages since, but I don't know what else to do about it. My heart is telling me to go to her and hold her in my arms, but my brain is telling me the opposite. That this was just a nice happy distraction for her and it didn't mean more than that."

"You don't really believe that do you?"

"I don't know what to believe, Pete." She ran her fingers through her hair in frustration. "I thought we were on the same page with our feelings, but now I'm not so sure. How could she just run away like that?" Her tone was becoming angrier with every word.

Peter sat back in his chair and looked thoughtful for a moment, as if choosing his words carefully. "Do you remember how devastated you were when your father passed away?" She looked up at him, fire in her eyes. He continued undaunted. "I do. You didn't eat for days on end; you hardly talked to anyone, barely left your room. And then when you finally did begin to emerge, you were so angry. You were mad at God, mad at everyone around you, mad at everything. The last time I had seen you acting out like that you were 9 years old and your mother had just left. Do you remember?" She just stared at her shoes and nodded almost imperceptibly. He leaned forward and placed his hand on hers to soften his words. "You have to remember that and put yourself in her shoes, Hailey. I know you feel some of what she's going through and I know you remember your own losses, but you had other people in your life that acted as your family- a lot of other people. It took a little while, but you snapped out of it, started coming back around. She will too."

"But why couldn't she have let me in? I would have been there for her, she knew that." She sighed and leaned heavily into the back of the couch.

"I can't speak to what motivates Elizabeth's heart, but it could have been any number of reasons that had nothing to do with her not loving you.

Everybody deals with these things in their own way, Hailey. And I know that right now, this feels like just another in a long line of loss for you, but give her some time. She just lost the only family she knew. It's going to take some time for her to reconcile that with how she viewed her life and her place in the world."

"I guess you're right, as usual." Her tone was one of defeat. "I just wish it didn't hurt so much."

"You really love her, don't you?" He sat back and eyed her thoughtfully. In all the years he'd known Hailey she had never lit up the way she did when she talked about Elizabeth. It was so palpable he could feel it all the way in California when they spoke on the phone.

"More than I've ever loved anyone, Peter."

"And do you think she loves you?"

"I thought so. I mean, God, Peter. When we made love it was transformative. Everything about being with her, whatever the context, it changed something vital in me for the better and I'd like to believe I did the same for her. I felt like we really connected, you know? But now..." She let her voice trail off into silence as she sat back into the warm embrace of her sofa.

"Well, I have to think that even though you didn't say the words that some part of her knows how you feel about her. And I know you're not completely blind or stupid so if you felt something deeper conveyed in your intimate moments then I have to believe you. Just give her some time. Let her know you're here, but back off and let her come to you. My guess is that she's hurting and scared and that if you push her, you probably won't get the result you're looking for."

Chapter 47

"Hi Elizabeth, we weren't expecting you to come in today." Jennifer stood to greet Elizabeth and wrapped her into a warm hug that lasted several moments. "I'm sure you're probably tired of people telling you how sorry they are for your loss, but in my case I know it's the truth and not just something you say at times like these." She held Elizabeth at arms length and looked at her appraisingly, taking note of the weight loss, the dark circles under her eyes, the slight slump to her posture, the casual clothes. "You look like hell. You wanna get some coffee and talk about it?" Jennifer offered her a tentative smile.

Elizabeth just shook her head and held back her tears. "No, I'm fine. But thank you Jennifer. You're a good person and a great friend and I'm sorry that we haven't had more time before to get to really get to know one another."

"Ok, now you're scaring me Elizabeth. Are you sure you're OK?" Concern was etched on her face.

Elizabeth let out a sort of laugh that sounded almost strangled and said, "Yea, I'm fine...Just realizing that life's too short not to let the people around you know how much you appreciate them. Is Harry in his office?"

For a second, the abrupt change in subject threw Jennifer, but she quickly recovered and gave Elizabeth a squeeze on her shoulder and let her know that Mr. Gordon was indeed in his office just then.

"Thanks. I have a few things to discuss with him, then I'm going back home." She gave Jennifer one last small smile and walked to her boss' office.

Chapter 48

"Well, I guess this is it. I miss you so much, Mom. I don't know how I'm going to get through it without you here to guide me, encouraging me, urging me to forge ahead." She held the silver urn containing Patty's ashes in her lap and looked out at the sprawling view spread out before her through the tears, taking in the bright autumn colors slashing themselves across the landscape in the morning sun. This had been their favorite place to hike and they had come together often when Elizabeth was younger. They had still managed it at least once a year when Elizabeth would visit, and it held a special place in both their hearts. *Now even more so than ever*, Elizabeth thought.

"It's been just over 3 months and I still can't believe you're actually gone. And after everything you went through to have finally seen the light at the end of the tunnel to have something as unexpected as a pulmonary embolus be the cause. Of all the things that could have gone wrong in the past several months to have it been something like that. I suppose I should be grateful that in the end it was quick and you probably didn't even feel it. I hope you didn't feel it, Mom. I suppose in time I'll see the silver lining there, but right now I just can't." She looked down at the silver dome lid of the pot and with her shirt sleeve she wiped the tears off of it.

"I'll take care of everything here, Mom. You don't have to worry. Maybe the change of pace will distract me and make me feel closer to you instead of reminding me that you're no longer here as you were before. 'Just changed shape is all,' right?

"I met Denise. She came to your life celebration and I finally got to meet her and her two children, Nathan and Nicole. When I saw her standing there, I thought I was seeing a ghost, Mom. She looks so much like you! You could have warned me, you know. I nearly had a heart attack. She showed me all the letters you had written her over the years and everything she had found regarding me too. It's strange to me how a family can say they care about each other while maintaining such a distance and never get together, never really share beyond just below the surface because someone was wrong and stubborn a long time ago. I suppose I should be thankful at the same time though because that same stubbornness resides in me and forces me to prove that I can when the world tells me I can't. I'm a lot like you in that way I guess."

She stood and opened the urn, looked in at the bits and pieces that remained of her mother's physical form. "OH! You were right about Hailey, Mom. I haven't had a chance to tell her yet, I mean besides every second that we've been together, but I do love her. I want to spend the rest of my life showing her just how much. I hope she'll have me after the way I left things. I was a mess when you died, Mom. I was scared, in pain and I just ran away from her without any explanation. I hope she can understand and forgive me. I'm still a mess, I'm still scared and I'm still in pain but at least now I have some purpose- some perspective. I guess I knew all along that this was the direction I would go…it just took some time for my heart to let my brain know. Thank you for that last push.

"So. A very wise woman once told me to 'live life' so that's what I'm going to do. The flesh may whither and die, but your spirit is very much alive in the hearts of the people you've touched and in the places you loved… To the earth I say please welcome this wise and wonderful woman, my mother, who loved and laughed and made so many things better simply by being. May you travel from this place without fear or worry, Mom. Be at Peace. I love you."

As the ashes poured from the urn a light breeze kicked up and carried the lighter parts high into the sky as though with one last flourish her mother was saying goodbye. Elizabeth stood there and watched for several minutes as the swirl spread down the slope and became part of the landscape. A feeling of utter peace overcame Elizabeth and for the first time in several weeks her heart felt light.

Chapter 49

Hailey was sitting on her patio drinking the first sips of coffee, watching Riley chasing butterflies in the mid morning sun when she heard a sound over her left shoulder. Riley must have heard it too because as her eyes followed him, he abandoned his mission and ran with purpose to Elizabeth who was crouched down giving him hugs and kisses. She nearly dropped her mug, but hid her surprise behind a guarded gaze.

"Hey there puppy, I missed you too." He was so excited that his whole body was wagging despite the strong embrace Elizabeth had him in, her face buried in his russet fur as she murmured to him. When she released him she stood and brushed the russet hairs from her clothes as best she could and looked up at Hailey, somewhat bashfully Hailey thought. *She looks good, Goddamned she's a sight for sore eyes.*

They stayed there for a long moment, seemly frozen in time. Hailey's heart was pounding in her chest so loudly that she was certain Elizabeth could hear it. *She came back! For how long? Why?*

"Hailey, hi." Elizabeth took a tentative step forward, wrung her hands at her waist.

"Hi." She stayed glued to her seat, afraid or unable to move.

"I tried knocking, but I guess you didn't hear me. I hoped I would catch you home." Elizabeth stood there looking uncertain.

"You could have called." Hailey was elated that Elizabeth had returned, but couldn't keep the hurt from her voice. Besides, she wasn't going to make it easy for her; not after just running off like that. She placed the coffee cup on the table next to her chair, hoping that Elizabeth didn't notice the tremor in her hand.

"You're right and I'm sorry. I could have called. I should have called." She took several more steps toward Hailey and stood before her looking like a woman with her heart on her sleeve. She plunged forward. "I should have done more than called, in fact. I should have stayed or taken you with me." Her eyes were imploring.

"Why?"

Taken aback at this response, her eyes widened and she stammered for a second. "I…Because…You…We…" She took a second to compose herself, shook her head and kneeled to better look Hailey in the eye. "Because I love you, Hailey. That's why I should have stayed or taken you with me or done more than left a note and a dog and run off. I was wrong to do that. It was fucked up. I was fucked up. I fucked up. But I love you and I want…I want…I just lost my mother I don't want to lose you too. I love you and I want to spend the rest of my life proving that to you, showing you. If you'll let me."

Hailey reached out and grabbed Elizabeth in a fierce embrace, pulling her into the chair with her and kissed her deeply. When they finally came up for air, Hailey continued to hold on to Elizabeth as though she were afraid to let her go, afraid she would run off again. "You can't ever do that again. You can't ever run away like that again, Elizabeth," she said emphatically, her voice breaking. "I thought you weren't going to come back. I thought I didn't mean anything to you. It broke my heart, Elle. You can't ever do that again. Next time things are fucked up you have to stay and we have to get through it together, OK?" Her body was shaking with emotion. Elizabeth just nodded her head and stood albeit shakily, offering a hand to Hailey. Hailey took it and allowed herself to be pulled up, where Elizabeth cupped her cheeks in both hands and wiped her tears away with her thumbs. She pulled Hailey into another hug and murmured to her.

"I'm so sorry Sweetheart. I never wanted to make you feel that way. I've been so blinded by my own pain that I didn't consider yours and I've been regretting it ever since. I love you Hailey Jensen and I am never going to run away again. I am going to be right here with you until we grow old and gray and past that even." She pulled back to search Hailey's eyes, "If that's what you want?"

"Yes." She kissed her, taking her lips with her own, sucking on the soft flesh, parting them with her tongue. "Yes, Elle. I love you so much I thought my soul was cracking when you left; I didn't think I would ever be whole again. I don't ever want to lose you." She kissed her again, deeply and they spent long moments getting reacquainted with each other. Each touching and grabbing at the other as though not believing they were really there.

"When do we leave for Boston?" Hailey asked when they broke apart again.

Elizabeth leaned back to look into Hailey's eyes and saw the seriousness there. "You want to move to Boston?"

Hailey looked back at her with confusion on her face. "That's where your life is, your job. I wouldn't take that away from you. I can do what I do from anywhere, and you're where my home is," she said seriously.

"Hailey, I love you dearly and thank you for that, but my life is here. With you, right here. I have a bakery to run, a dog to raise, canvasses that need paint and a satellite branch of Gordon Phillips to launch. So you see we can't move to Boston. Besides, I've already rented my place out."

Shocked, it was Hailey's turn to stammer, "Wha…When?"

Elizabeth laughed and kissed Hailey again, who just looked at her lover in amazement. "Before Mom died, I had no idea how long I'd be staying here and when I finally admitted to myself how madly in love with you I was falling I knew I had to do something. So I pitched the idea to Harry Gordon one day. The Denver area puts us in good position to tap into both the West Coast and Midwestern markets, as well as several emerging possibilities in the Southwest. The name will attract good talent, as will the area, and I'll be a full partner. We've already got 10 people on board from the main office ready to get it started; they're all capable people and can handle most of it without me." She shrugged. "I went to Boston to attend to those details and arrange for my things." She smiled and shrugged as she continued. "If it doesn't work out or it all takes too much from me or from us, well…Mom did really well with the bakery so I know I will too, and she had a nice savings and I've got my savings and a prime piece of real estate already rented out at a premium in Boston, so I'm not worried about it. You seem to have a successful thing going for yourself so I'm not worried about you in that respect. I think everything will be fine however it works out. Life's way too short to sweat the small stuff, right?"

Hailey didn't think she could love Elizabeth any more than she already did but somehow the feeling grew and blossomed in her chest even more than she thought possible and that's saying something since she was already on uncharted ground. "Will you marry me? I mean, I know that we can't in Colorado, but I have a team of lawyers that can take care of the legalities." She was starting to ramble and reined it in before she gave too much away too soon. "Will you marry me, Elizabeth?"

"Isn't that essentially what I just asked you?" She grinned. "Of course I'll marry you, Hailey. I love you with all my heart and soul. I can already promise you that I will spend the rest of my life loving you. In fact..." She pulled a velvet box from the pocket of her hooded sweatshirt and opened it as she knelt and presented it to Hailey. The ring was simple, understated, 3 carats of diamond embedded into a platinum channel band with an inscription inside that read *my life, my love*.

"I figured with the work you do, something in a more traditional feminine setting would just get in the way. This is low profile, so I figure it would be safer." Elizabeth rushed on.

Beyond words, Hailey got on her knees as well and relayed her response with a searing kiss that sent them both into the stratosphere.

"Wait...Wait." She fought to catch her breath. "There's something I need to tell you," Hailey said, albeit breathlessly. "If you're going to marry me, there's something you need to know about me." Suddenly she was nervous, not because she had bad news, but because she had deceived Elizabeth- even if the reasons were good. Elizabeth was looking at her with a mixture of jubilation and confusion.

"What is it, Love?" Her expression became one of concern. "You can tell me anything, you know. I'm not going to pull away if you tell me you have half a million dollars in credit card debt or that you were arrested for possession or something like that." She reached up and swept a wayward strand of Hailey's ebony hair from her face and cupped her cheek.

Hailey laughed, "No. No it's nothing like that. It's something really good, I think. Keep in mind that it's something that's been true for me my whole life and when people find out they change around me, or if they know in advance it seems to be the reason they like me, which is why I'm so secretive about it now that I'm older and wiser."

Elizabeth tried to shrug off the uneasy feeling and laughed nervously, "So, what? Are you insanely rich or something then?"

Hailey just smiled at her, her eyes sparkling as she searched Elizabeth's for understanding.

Elizabeth's jaw dropped. "Oh. My. God. It was you, wasn't it? With the hospital and the donation."

Hailey just nodded and kept her amused expression as she watched Elizabeth figure it all out.

"You're *that* Jensen? JII? Holy shit, no wonder you keep that a secret!" She sat back on her heels, stunned, looking at Hailey in awe of the news; this beautiful, down to earth, downright humble woman was one of the top 10 richest women in the country and she had had no idea whatsoever. She was floored, and then she realized what Hailey had mentioned about why people seemed to like her. An idea struck her.

"I'll sign a pre-nup." She rushed on, "Right now, I'll sign it. I don't want your money, Hailey. I only want you and if you had nothing I'd still love you forever." She told her emphatically and urgently as she cupped Hailey's cheeks in her palms and looked deep into her eyes again. "In fact, I insist on it. I don't want you to ever wonder why I'm with you or why I stay. I'm with you because I love you and I stay because I can't bear to be without you. I won't marry you without one, but I'll still stay with you and love you forever as partners if you try to be more stubborn than me on this."

All Hailey could do just then was kiss her again. And again. And again. Until they found themselves sprawled across Hailey's bed, a tangled mass of sweaty heaving bodies struggling not to fall asleep in the aftermath of mutual euphoria.

Epilogue

Two Years Later

The First Annual Patty Thornton Memorial Weekend of Healing – a 60 mile bike ride, a 3, 5 and 10K race/walk, and sidewalk fair to honor Patty and raise awareness and money for AML research went off without a hitch. Several thousand participants in the various events who flew in from all over the country as well as most of the locals enjoyed music, food and camaraderie to raise nearly a half million dollars for finding a cure for AML. Local businesses sponsored tents and donated prizes, the local hospitality industry provided cut rate rooms for the participants and several local bands donated a few hours of playing time to provide some entertainment.

"I can't believe how well this turned out! Look at all these people!" Elizabeth turned to Hailey with a look of pleased awe.

"Of course it turned out so well, Darling- you were the driving force behind it." She gave Elizabeth a wide smile, her eyes were sparkling and kissed her temple as she draped an arm over her shoulder and gave her a squeeze.

"Well, I had the love of a good woman too, a very beautiful and wonderful woman whom I absolutely adore. Thank you for helping me put this together, Hailey. I don't think I could have done it without you." She turned into Hailey's embrace and wrapped her arms around her waist.

Hailey blushed at the praise and leaned into a

sweet kiss. "You know…I was thinking that this will probably be even bigger next year, what with everyone from this year telling all their friends what a great time it was and so on. Maybe we could get a bigger name to play it out- a headliner even. I was also thinking the area could use a couple more places for people to stay when this thing totally explodes…I mean, every single one of the local hotels is overflowing and there are several tracts of land I've been thinking might be a great place to put some sort of accommodations on… maybe cabins or something like that…we could rent them out to the tourists when this isn't the priority." She raised a hand and swept it around indicating the event.

"You'd do that?" Hailey never ceased to amaze Elizabeth. Her generosity was astounding and inspiring.

"Of course I would, Sweetheart. Not only would it be good business for the tourism side of it, but it would be another great way to support the event."

"I love you, Hailey Jensen. You are the most amazing and wonderful woman and I feel so lucky to have found you."

"I love you too Sweetheart and I could say all the same things about you." They kissed a lingering kiss that left them both smiling and light headed.

"Hey there you are!" Charlie and Diane walked up to them and they exchanged hugs of greeting between them.

"I see you brought Madison with you. She is getting so big!" Hailey reached out a finger to the baby sitting in the carrier strapped to Charlie's upper body and proceeded to engage the 8 month old girl in a game of coochie-coo much to Madison's squealing delight.

"So when are you two finally going to slow down

enough to have kids?" Charlie teased them.

Hailey just looked at Elizabeth with a devilish grin and said, "Whenever she's ready."

Elizabeth looked a bit surprised, "You want kids? You never told me that."

"Well, we could definitely talk about it if you want. I mean, I love the life we have and the freedom and all of that, but I would like to have a family with you someday. Not this second, but maybe someday."

"I'd like that too. One from me and one from you, we can even swap if you want." She gave Hailey a devilish grin of her own, "I bet Peter would make a great donor, too."

Hailey was taken aback at the level of contemplation Elizabeth had seemingly put into this. "So have you been thinking about this long?"

"Not too long, I guess." She winked at Charlie and Diane who were watching this exchange in amusement. "Only since Diane announced that she was pregnant with Madison."

"What? Why didn't you say anything, Sweetheart?" She turned to Charlie, "Did you have any idea about all this?"

He just grinned and shrugged.

"I didn't mention it because you didn't and we had a lot going on. But Sweetheart, if this is something you want, I'd gladly have a family with you."

"I love you so much, Elle." She took her in her arms and gave her a big hug and a kiss. When she let go she was excited. "Let's go find Peta!"

ABOUT THE AUTHOR

As an only child, Kathleen Wheeler spent most of her childhood in southwestern New Mexico splitting her time between her parent's house and the cattle ranch where her mother grew up. She is a student of life and a bit of a nomad as well as a Jane of all trades, having lived in 9 states and 2 countries and working all manner of jobs. She has been an all night gas station attendant, a car washer, coffee slinger, landscaper, radio news writer, potter and studio manager, dog food rep, café manager, chef's assistant, dishwasher, she was even a fancy corporate sales executive working with top high tech companies and most recently became a content developer and blogger for her family's websites GenWed.com and AllFreeRecords.com as well as being a part time mother to a beautiful son whom she adores with everything she has.

She plays several musical instruments, loves to create anything- especially if it makes a mess, enjoys cooking, reading, film, hiking, kayaking and mountain biking and generally anything that involves going outside.

Ms. Wheeler started writing at an early age and has found ways throughout her life to keep it up, despite the fact that *Changing Shape* (2012) is her first substantial work of fiction. Early published work includes poetry and various newspaper articles; more recent work consists of trade papers and marketing content for various clients (blog and websites notwithstanding).

She reads an obscene amount of books, has recently digitized her library in order to have room for living, and she currently calls Birmingham Alabama home (for now).

You can make contact with her through her Facebook profile https://www.facebook.com/katwheelerbooks , Twitter @ https://twitter.com/KatWheelerBooks or via email @ katwheelerbooks@gmail.com or follow her blog @ katwheelerbooks.blogspot.com

www.ingramcontent.com/pod-product-compliance
Lightning Source LLC
Chambersburg PA
CBHW031304170626
46807CB00001B/297